Noida Express

Jitendra Anand

website: jai3e.wordpress.com

ISBN No. "978-81-939444-0-0"

Published by:

M/s Jitendra Anand Infratech Private Limited, 2203, Express Trade Towers – 2, Sector – 132, Noida – 201304. e-mail: jaipl3e@gmail.com

Acknowledgements

I never imagined I had be an author some day. Last year, I was given an assignment to write a technical book for the Ministry of Rural Development, while working for them as a consultant. That experience triggered the passion for writing inside me. Now with each passing day, I feel happy and am determined to pursue writing in my life.

I thank my wife Pooja, a constant inspiration and motivation, irrespective of all difficulties in life,for always being there for me. And my children, Rohit and Dhara, for always reminding me to keep moving in this direction, with their words of encouragement.

I am grateful to friends and colleagues, who supported me with kind words and quotes of inspiration. And last, but not the least, all of you. I feel inspired to work harder.

I am feeling blessed after visiting Mahakaaleshwar Jyotirlinga today for the first time.

ॐमहाकालमहाकाय, महाकालजगत्पते।
महाकालमहायोगिनः, महाकालनमोस्तुते॥

JAI HO MAHADEV.

17th August, 2018, Ujjain

Jitendra Anand

20th May 2018

New Delhi Railway Station

Sumit Bhatnagar was relieved while boarding the Puri Express. The train was on time. Sumit kept his luggage securely under the seat, got down and went straight to a tea seller. The aroma of hot tea, as he took his first sip, woke him up. Today, he would be leaving the city, never to return and there would be no place like Noida in his dictionary forever. He would take a break in the remote jungles of Koraput in Odisha, live with unknown villagers and disappear from city life for some time.

The train gave a quick siren at 7 o'clock in the morning. Sumit was sitting by the window and the air smelt like heaven.

The Puri Express started and picked up momentum, the platform getting left behind.

He saw a lady in a blue sari and a medium-sized handbag hanging from her left shoulder, holding a bouquet of yellow roses in her hand.

As the train moved, her face came closer to him and with it, bewilderment in his eyes. While crossing the electric pole, Sumit realised the danger, he wanted to lie down immediately. The lady smiled as he looked at her for a fleeting moment.

He tried to bring his head down quickly, almost jumping off the seat.

There was no sound, but he felt a vibration in his chest. Within seconds there was pain and next followed a cardiac arrest.

Sumit was still seeing the smile on her face, the face left behind the speeding train.

He knew what had happened and also the fact that he'd live for another five to six minutes. He clutched his chest with pain. He saw that his fellow passengers were busy with their little daughter and did not notice anything.

Sumit crumbled with pain in his chest, his heart started pumping as if in a sprint race.

He spoke no words, sought no help, no agony, no more explanations and no regret. This time he decided to accept fate and closed his eyes.

Sumit felt the rupture of veins in his heart and his hands fell down as his body slipped down from the seat.

His fellow passengers jumped towards him in panic. They started talking loudly and screamed for a doctor, shaking him and calling him.

The ticket checker came running to the scene. As the railway station was still nearby, the passengers asked the ticket checker to stop the train immediately.

By the time the train came to a halt, New Delhi Railway Station was almost a kilometre behind.

*

The young woman was on her way to Noida. There was silence in the car as her father slowly manoeuvred in the traffic.

'Noida Express', the prime witness of the crime one year ago, followed them slowly at a distance.

Her mother, who was eagerly waiting, jumped to the door with questioning eyes.

There was silence on the face of her daughter.

She found it difficult to control her tears; it was 8:15 in the morning, time for breakfast and time to leave for office and college. No one uttered a single word, after a quick breakfast they packed their lunch and left.

It was yet another day in the busy life of NCR.

ONE YEAR AGO

19th May 2017

Noida

1.

Ankita Sharma walked slowly towards her house in Sector-51, Noida - a multi-storey apartment, Suntech Heights, almost 8 kms from Mahamaya flyover. Her house was on the 12th floor on the open side, giving a hazy view of the surrounding area as always because of dust in the city. It seldom rained in Noida, but whenever it rained even for an hour, the clear view of far away high-rise multi-storied buildings gave a different and majestic view of the skyline.

Noida, the city of aspirations for thousands, slowly expanded into a twin city with Greater Noida, the intercity space turning into a concrete jungle with hundreds of residential and office complexes.

She was pursuing her Masters in Physics at the Government College, Sector 39, Noida under Chaudhary Charan Singh University, Meerut. The college was close to her house and very conveniently located. It was the distance that made Ankita to choose this college. In spite of being intelligent and getting good marks in 12th class and in graduation, she was not keen on joining a prestigious college. Her dream and approach to life were very different.

Her passion was for a simple concept—how much time could she set aside for her pursuit of knowledge in the subject of sounds, vibrations, oscillations, resonances and its connection with Vedic sciences, literature and knowledge of the ancient times, and experimenting with the simple electronic gadgets that she was so fond of making at home. A room, converted into a mini lab was dedicated to all her pursuits, full of books, wires, tiny devices, computers, all containing paraphernalia that no one else understood.

It was a long debate with her parents that finally ended in a decision. She would pursue a doctorate in sound from some prestigious college or university, but only after finishing her post-graduation here. Living with her mother was her top priority; nothing else mattered.

Ankita was a shy and extraordinary girl, envied by many of her classmates, who used to buckle under simple questions. To find a peer group on the level of Ankita was difficult; her level of knowledge created a sense of respect amongst the professors in the college. She earned a special place in the eyes of Dr. Jatin Agnihotri, Associate Professor and HOD of the Physics Department. He was a lean, bespectacled man of short stature.

Dr. Jatin was a special case. His father, a schoolteacher, barely managed to educate his two sons and a daughter while fighting for the survival of his family. Jatin tutored students to finance his education during graduation and post-graduation days. His worries ended when he received a scholarship while pursuing PhD.

Dr. Jatin had been brilliant in his student days; his love for physics mesmerized his father too. His father was sure that one day Jatin would be an eminent personality while leading a respectable life. When Jatin told his father about getting admission for a doctorate from Banaras Hindu University, his joy knew no bounds. The chances of Jatin becoming a Professor someday brought tears of happiness to his eyes.

After completing his doctorate, Jatin joined a private engineering college to teach applied sciences and after three years there, managed to qualify as an Assistant Professor in the Government College at Noida. It was now his twelfth year of service and with one promotion he had become an Associate Professor and had published more than twenty research papers in prestigious journals that had earned a name for him in literary circles.

When he met Ankita, a silent girl in his class, he was a little amused. She was different from her classmates, generally engrossed in some book and not so talkative. All assignments were submitted on time and generally hundred percent correct answers to mock tests or semester examinations. With time, she earned a sense of respect from Dr. Jatin.

During discussions with her, he came to know about her interest in sounds, vibrations and its effect on bodies and minds.

One day he told her, 'The whole world is a sound, universe is manifestation of sound, every moving body has a sound, from subatomic particles revolving around the nucleus to plants, animals, human actions, moving cars, planets, stars, and even the Milky Way has a sound. Now, when science has been able to capture the electromagnetic waves into mechanical waves, we can listen to the sounds of faraway stars and galaxies.'

Dr. Jatin continued, 'By capturing the electromagnetic radiation of the Sun, one can now listen to sounds of the Sun and even study the actions and reactions inside the Sun. Someday, people will listen to the vibrations of bodies and understand the reasons inside for the causes of illnesses and miseries.'

Dr. Jatin was always helpful and courteous, he welcomed Ankita for any random discussion, using up his free time and even solved queries while advising further reference materials on her favourite topics.

Her mother, Manju was running a viral fever and her father Santosh Sharma was on official tour, most likely to return after three days. She bought a packet of bread, some vegetables and milk. The doctor had prescribed rest and medicines, but the fever was not coming down. Ankita reported to her father about the progress of her mother's recovery every morning and evening.

As usual, the calm and relaxed voice of her father was more than any medicine. Ankita never failed to appreciate and love her father, a man of medium build, bespectacled and studious looking. He was an easy-going person and had been a brilliant student of physics in his college days. Ankita inherited the love for science from him. He was also very fond of ancient literature and tried to find the interrelations of modern physics with metaphysics. By the time Ankita was 21 years old, she had imbibed many of his traits — the intuitive mind and craving for experiments, searching for new concepts and relating it with theories in mythology.

Manju sometimes felt frustrated by the conversations between daughter and father and used to escape to watch television, a little worried about who would marry her philosophical daughter?

'What would you like to eat?' Ankita asked her mother.

As usual, her mother was lost in her favourite serial. Ankita called her mother again but there was no reply.

Ankita stood in between her mother and the television, 'First tell me, sandwich, simple bread butter or any other snack?'

Manju grinned. Her daughter was very caring, like her father, seldom getting angry.

'Ok dear, make me a toast with hot milk, I am alright now, don't worry,' Manju smiled at her daughter.

'Sure, mummy', Ankita went to the kitchen to prepare it and after half an hour joined her mother.

Breakfast served, Manju and her daughter were laughing at a drama serial on television. Together, they sat on the shiny, light brown sofa set. Manju looked at Ankita, and once again, she was lost in watching the TV.

The next serial on television started.

'Are you not tired of watching TV?' Ankita asked her in a stern voice.

'Ok, I will switch it off after this serial.' Manju smiled at her.

2.

Ankita heaved a sigh of relief. After giving her mother medicines, she returned to her room. It was time for guided meditation, another normal Saturday.

Ankita closed her eyes and started her exercises. The sound of deep breathing and chanting of AUM started resonating in the room. After her daily routine, she gazed again at the graphics on the wall that she had done:

'The more precisely the position is determined, the less precisely the momentum or velocity is known in this instant, and vice versa.'

Any attempt to measure precisely the velocity of a subatomic particle, will knock it about in an unpredictable way, so that a simultaneous measurement of its position has no validity and it arises out of the intimate connection in nature between particles and waves in the realm of subatomic dimensions.

- Werner Heisenberg, 1927

It was a well-known principle and she read it hundreds of times, but the reason was different because of her interests. Did Heisenberg's uncertainty principle affect the thoughts occurring in the mind? Could it be applied to resonance, oscillations and effects of sound on objects?

A weird, wild and utopian idea, yes it was. When Ankita conveyed this to her father for the first time, he laughed with gusto.

'You know Ankita, sometimes the seemingly most utopian thought can do wonders, after all who knows the truth? What the mind can imagine may become possible in the universe. We don't know many things in life.' He remembered this day for the wild thoughts of his daughter for a long time and used to smile at the poster, neatly framed and fixed on the wall.

For Ankita, it was a dream research topic, the pursuit of ancient science written in mythologies, interwoven principles of modern physics with sound as specific domain, was her best utilization of time.

And time was aplenty when compared with what her life would have been had she joined any of those far away colleges and institutes, with their rigorous schedules or commuting to Delhi every day. Even staying in a hostel and being part of everyday chores of a nerve wrecking busy lifestyle wouldn't have suited her.

3.

Nandkishor received a call from his native place, Mewla Gopalgarh near Jewar, a small village situated on the way side of a minor road connecting Hamirpur to Tappal.

The easiest way to reach there was to take a route on the expressway and turn left near Jewar. The single lane road merged with Palwal-Aligarh road. Agricultural fields and mango farms on both sides of the village road made the area lush and green and it resembled a small forest.

The engagement ceremony of Nandkishor's elder brother's daughter was fixed with a boy from a nearby village. There was some urgency as the groom's side wanted to complete the ring ceremony this week itself.

His elder brother called Nandkishor along with his family to help in arranging for the engagement function. His son, Rahul Kumar, used to accompany him on these occasions, but he was on the way to Gorakhpur for some catering work at a function and he was not expected to return shortly.

4.

Nandkishor was a simple man, not formally educated and came from a very humble background. He had decided to shift to Noida from his village for the sake of employment and survival. His family hardly managed to earn a decent living. He finally decided to come to Noida to make a foray in the street-food business as the family belonged to a long line of street food sellers.

Nandkishor realised that with little investment in Noida, he could survive with his family by selling snacks on the streets near some offices. Young professionals, flocking in large groups, were working in corporate offices in Sector–62. There was a huge demand for breakfast and lunch as many of them were bachelors, unable to cook or mostly used to take lunch at street food outlets due to lack of time.

He borrowed some money and purchased a rickshaw cart, cooking ingredients and utensils. His wife, Sujata too joined him.

On the very first day, when they started selling, business rocketed and both of them couldn't believe it. The profit was respectable, much more than the entire week's earnings back home.

Nandkishor became more determined. He rented a house with a big kitchen in Mamura, the most affordable area near Sector-62. He found some more people from his village, Mewla Gopalgarh and nearby villages in Jewar with many more coming from far off places for the sake of employment. These workers were mainly employed in factories as technicians, electricians, construction workers, vendors and rickshaw pullers. They formed the endless inflow in the densely populated urban village of Mamura in Noida.

The village Mamura in the heart of the city is a very congested place beyond imagination. The sky rocketing land prices and surge of housing projects did not spare any respectable yet cheap place for poor workers. The perspective planning, with emphasis on vertical growth, left no consideration for the economically weaker sections of the society, and it really created a mess in the city.

With the cost of living much more than their earning for a majority of the people, Noida had become a nightmare of diaspora with its reckless development. The planning authority had ignored the welfare of people by selling the land pockets to developers, who extracted money from people and did not deliver. With no land parcels left to accommodate the needy lower strata of the society, many migrants like Nandkishor were forced to live in congested villages under unhygienic conditions.

Nandkishor finally succeeded in leading a tough but economically sustainable life along with his wife, son Rahul Kumar and daughter Sakshi.

Six years go by in Noida selling street food to office-going professionals. The twelve-year-old son and seven-year-old daughter at the time of shifting from village to the city of thousands of aspirations were now eighteen and thirteen years old.

5.

Surender Nagar was quite a dashing personality. His father was a politically influential teacher with affiliations in the ruling party. Teja Nagar was a well-known figure in Hamirpur and the surrounding area.

Every day party people used to come to Teja's doorsteps to invite him to functions. Such was his influence among local villagers that his endorsement of a candidate could swing thousands of votes.

Teja never desired a political position and remained a benevolent worker at the grass root level. When Surender reached the age of twenty-six years, his father was worried about his job. He wanted a safe career for Surender, but somehow his hard-working son, meritorious in his own way, could not qualify for the UPSC or State PSC competitions. He always wished that his son should qualify for the Civil Services Examination and Surender also prepared hard, appeared all the four times, but somehow failed either in the interviews or due to an overall low score.

Teja was a worried man. He knew it was not so easy to qualify for the national level competitions. His son could not get the employment that he wished.

Finally, Teja decided to take political help and met Hem Pratap Singh, the Chief Minister in Lucknow. The Chief Minister was surprised with his request; the backbone of his political party in his constitutional area was asking for a little help.

Hem Pratap called Ved Prakash Dagar, Director General of Police of his state, Uttar Pradesh for a meeting. There had been similar requests from affiliated stalwarts of the party and the Chief Minister wanted to help and build support for his cronies, providing employment in the state police service was the easiest. Finally, the total requests were counted and after taking other category vacancies into consideration, the Chief Minister allowed recruitment of one hundred and fourteen inspectors in the state police through open competition.

The State Public Service Commission followed the procedures and completed all the formalities, and exams were conducted with due diligence.

Surender also appeared with other candidates. This time, he could qualify for the exams, courtesy of his father, as all the exam papers had reached him a week in advance.

Surender joined the Police Services as an Inspector the following year. No doubt, he was brilliant and hardworking but somehow luck needed some tweaks to strike.

Hem Pratap Singh, the Chief Minister knew how to take political advantage of it, he needed many persons like him for crisis management and he gave them full support, even going out of the way and circumventing the systems. After all, exigencies keep arriving at odd moments and the police was the best help for formidable political factors and rivals.

6.

Bholaram Yadav, the sub-inspector in charge of the area was a little late due to some personal work. The best principle Bholaram knew was earning a decent salary and serving his family. His love for food was well known in his circle, and the best part of the story was that he always ensured that friends enjoyed famous delicacies of the area as many times as possible.

His popularity grew like a fruit bearing tree. Name a famous shop and he knew it. If anyone asked about a food item, he could guide them to the best shop. Distance never mattered, be it in a gypsy, car, motorcycle; he was ever ready to bring the delicacies whenever any senior officer came to his area. He knew many officers by the flavours they enjoyed, including their wives' choices.

Bholaram was a different person altogether, unlike many of his counterparts involved in murky practices; he stayed away from the filth. He was very keen on providing quality education to his two sons, Shobhit and Shubham and the boys did not let their parents down.

His elder son, Shobhit was brilliant and always wanted to study computer science since childhood. He was hard working and meritorious, qualifying for the JEE Mains exams in the first attempt itself with a good rank. He could not make it to an IIT, but still managed to get his favourite subject from National Institute of Technology, Jaipur.

The younger son, the mother's favourite decided to remain in Noida and joined Greater Noida Engineering College for B.Tech in Mechanical Engineering.

Bholaram, the honest police officer and his dedicated wife and homemaker, Sumita were satisfied with the performance of their children, and preferred to live a quiet and peaceful life. In a world full of cutthroat competition and prevailing trends of children of his colleagues, they were happy.

It had been a leap after a generation's hard work when coming from a remote village in Hamirpur, Bholaram had been selected as a constable in the State Police Service some 24 years ago at the age of twenty-one years and was gradually promoted to become a Sub-Inspector.

7.

Ankita slowly opened her eyes from her daily meditation. She rested on the choir mat for some more time with her spine erect, it was a little different today. She had been practising for almost five years now, but today she felt like she was receiving vibrations from unknown sources.

Ankita tried to ignore it but sensed the rhythm of her heart.

Santosh, on tour, called her, surprisingly asking about the daily events. She told her father, who was also her best friend, about the day's happenings.

Santosh laughed, 'Go to the kitchen, make a cup of coffee for mother and yourself, and ask her what she would like to have for lunch.'

It was another day as usual, her mom watching her favourite serial on TV and her father returning home from official tour to Jaisalmer.

With two cups of coffee, Ankita joined her mother to watch the show.

8.

Ankita asked her mother if she was feeling well. Manju replied that she was feeling much better. Ankita was relieved and prepared her mother's favourite dishes.

Her mother was a little tired due to her prolonged mild viral fever and went to sleep. The next day, after taking her lunch Ankita again headed for her room and sat on the chair staring at the almirah filled with books.

In front of her was a large collection of books on modern physics, Vedas, Upanishads and metaphysics, a collection of spiral bound books that she had meticulously downloaded, presentations on effects of sound on objects, hundreds of research papers, downloaded experiments of sound moving objects, vibrations and their effect, all those read in the last five years.

For Ankita it was not a matter of studying the facts in the books but an aspiration to understand the relations, analysing them and then experimenting.

She kept reading verses from one of the Upanishads and moved to another book. Trying to look forthe logic behind chanting of mantras in wars, sounds, effect of natural forces in wars between kings and demons.

9.

Ankita had a room dedicated to her studies and experiments as Santosh had been supportive of her pursuits since her childhood. The room had a three feet wide long table for the full length of wall, cupboards and drawers under the table to keep wires, cables, transistors, microprocessors, hundreds of speakers, tuning forks of many sizes, capacitors and transducers among other things. Some of the items had even been imported from Europe and Japan for specific needs.

Santosh Sharma invested a lot of money in his daughter so that she could experiment in her free time. It was a facility that her friends and relatives envied. What was the need for spending so much money and how many cared for any results and research? The father-daughter relationship was very different from that of the rest of the crowd.

Ankita made many small devices with her knowledge and inquisitive nature. A few of the devices on recording sounds were taken up by local manufacturers for production. In the five years of her venturingin to the mini lab at home, she had developed a network of suppliers and vendors for cost-effective material needed for her experiments.

10.

Krishna Nagar met Bholaram Yadav through Surendra Nagar's wife; she was overwhelmed by their courtesy and behaviour. She almost felt like she was on top of the world with the courtesy of a variety of dishes served. Sumita Yadav flattered her during her three days' stay in Noida.

Bholaram as usual never failed to tell stories to Krishna about shops, special food crafts, locations with delicacies of nearby areas. Variety was his speciality and the weakness of many.

11.

Nandkishor called his neighbour, Suresh Kumar, an electrician of around twenty-one years of age who was from a nearby village. For the last few days, Nandkishor had been eager to visit his village.

Suresh easily agreed to accompany him during the visit.

'How will you go?' Suresh asked Nandkishor.

'Well, my wife and daughter also want to go with me. With you, there will be four persons, should we hire a taxi?' he asked.

Suresh immediately asked, 'My friend drives a Maruti Eeco, will it serve the purpose?'

'Yes, first class,' Nandkishor's problem was solved.

Suresh immediately called Rajpal, again a local driver from his village who had been driving a taxi in Noida for the last five years and stayed in Mamura itself.

Rajpal belonged to a poor family; he started earning while serving as a helper at the age of fourteen years on a small freight carrier in his village. Tata Magic was the bread and butter and the driver was a kind person. For five years, he worked with him, going from place to place, loading and unloading single-handedly.

It was after many trips to Noida for transporting, mostly vegetables from his village, that he decided to shift to Noida. He learned driving while being a helper and easily got a job as a taxi driver for a local tour operator.

As years passed, his earnings improved and he finally took a decision to purchase a Maruti Eeco, to ferry goods and run as a taxi. It made more financial sense to get a Maruti Eeco and not any other vehicle in the same price range. Eeco, a multi-purpose vehicle, changed roles easily, from shared taxi to ferrying small household items.

Rajpal, with all his love and care, named his Maruti Eeco,'Noida Express', written boldly on the front and rear, visible from a distance. The name got publicity and attention from clients and travellers; who remembered it for a long time.

It was agreed that they would all travel in the evening to Mewla Gopalgarh, which was just 110 km away from Noida and hardly two to two and a half hour's journey. Even if they started the journey at 8:00 p.m. they would reach their destination by 10:30 p.m. Rajpal's wife also decided to accompany them.

Nandkishor, his wife Sujata and daughter Sakshi, Suresh Kumar, Rajpal and his wife Kasturi Devi, a total of six people left for Mewla Gopalgarh by 'Noida Express', the beloved Maruti Eeco of Rajpal.

12.

Ankita was not just curious about her passion, she was obsessed with the subject of sounds and vibrations. She always fancied that someday she would be able to make a device that worked on the concept of vibrations of her sound to move external objects. She was convinced due to all those evidences drawn from ancient mythologies and number of scriptures. The more she read the ideas, the more she tried to relate it with basic concepts of physics.

She calculated the timelines of various characters and the battles with all the mythological characters, redrafted the concept of the time several times and while matching with the time period of Surya Siddhant by Mayasur at 6778 BC, she reached the time when Lord Indra, the God of rains and thunderstorms, fought with Vritrasura around 13650 BC using verses and quotes in Vedanga Jyotish and star positions of related hymns of the epic fight in Rig Veda.

'What happened at that time?' she was again lost in her thoughts. The battle was not a normal battle; it involved the use of nature in the most violent manner. How were they really controlled?

Ankita tried to deflect the idea from her mind. What to read further? She again opened a chapter on the travel of vibrations of sound and resonance.

It was dinnertime. Manju knocked at the door, Ankita rushed out. Her mom was smiling at her again as she was lost in the books.

'No one will marry such a bookworm of a girl,' Manju teased her.

'I will stay with you for ever, I don't want to go anywhere', Ankita repeated her answer.

Manju was a little better now, and decided to cook a meal for Ankita and herself.

Ankita went to the kitchen to help her and switched on the music system gifted by her dad to Manju on her last birthday. The kitchen filled with sounds of old songs. Manju smiled.

13.

Krishna Nagar was very happy to visit Noida. Would it be possible that her husband gets transferred here from Hamirpur, her sleepy and small hometown?

The matter was discussed with her husband and he agreed to apply for a transfer. The IG of Police was quite happy with him, due to his performance and supported him most of the time. He had a discussion with Ved Prakash Dagar, DGP about the posting and luck smiled.

Surender was transferred to Noida within a month of dreaming about it with his wife. Krishna felt very happy. After all, she was a lucky person with political influence because of her well-connected father-in-law, Teja Nagar, the man with the right contacts in the ruling party.

14.

Ankita returned to her room at 8 p.m., she still had two hours left before her bed time. Her routine started at five in the morning with one-hour yoga and meditation.

Looking at the digital clock on the wall, Ankita wondered what to do. Her mother had gone to sleep straight after dinner.

'What to do now?' Ankita stared at the book shelves -books on physics and more physics and scriptures, hundreds of them, all properly stacked in five cupboards.

She finally decided to read the story of Vritrasura once more.

After getting defeated by Asuras, the Devas approached Lord Brahma, who advised them to approach Vishwarupa, the son of Tvasta, saying, 'Vishwarupa will fulfil your desires but he is also inclined to favour the Asuras.'

After listening to the request of the Devas, Vishwarupa gave King Indra the Narayan Kavach and narrated the detailed methodology to perform the rituals, that the syllables should be chanted with extreme care, the positive armour of the mantra will then personify in all directions. Supreme Lord Vishnu's names, transcendental forms, his weapons, his intelligence, mind, life and air will protect you from all kinds of dangers.

Vishwarupa concluded, 'The Narayana Kavach will enable you to conquer your enemies, the demons. You will conquer disease and venom, Asuras, ammunition of thousand atomic bombs, no weapon will harm you. May the wrath of Lord Shiva protect you all.'

However, Vishwarupa had a soft corner for the Asuras and kept on helping them. Once King Indra got to know how Vishwarupa was helping the Asuras and cheating the Devas and he killed him out of fear.

Tvasta became very angry upon hearing of his son Vishwarupa's death, and he performed a specific yagna for the purpose of killing Indra.

While chanting, Tvasta offered, "O enemy of Indra, flourish to kill your foe without delay!"

However, Tvasta in his rage pronounced incorrectly.'Indra-shatro' means 'enemy of Indra'. Tvasta mistakenly said 'Indra-shatro', making the change in vibrations and frequency sound of the longer 'aa' and the meaning changed to 'Indra, who is an enemy'.

Ankita was deep in thought, trying to relate the vibrations and oscillations, the sounds of chanting and how a wrong pronunciation could have brought destruction to his son, she kept on reading.

Vritrasura, born from the fire of yagna was a terrific demon, a great Asura. Like the meaning of his name, Vritrasura covered the entire planetary system, controlled the rivers, becoming the destroyer of all creation; he made the whole world tremble with fear. He became a mighty king of the Asuras, everyone ran in all directions to save their lives. Vritrasura resorted to violence against the Devas.

When every effort of theirs failed, King Indra was advised to approach Rishi Dadhichi, to make the weapon 'Vajra' from his bones. After considering the request, the great Rishi left his earthly abode to help the Devas.

'Vajra' was capable of launching a thunderstorm with lightning, when infused with the power of mantras chanted by Lord Vishnu.

This battle took place on the banks of river Narmada between the Asuras and the Devas. The sky and earth were filled with shattering sounds of lighting, thunderbolts and weapons.

Vritrasura's trident struck Indra like a meteorite, but King Indra crushed it with his 'Vajra' powered by thousands of thunderbolts of lightning in the sky and finally killed Vritrasura.

Ankita was once again overwhelmed by the fine details of warfare techniques in the story, her mind again going deep into the world of vibrations, sounds, resonances, recitations and projecting waves in a particular direction for creation or destruction. Vibrations were used everywhere in the epic fight.

For her, the great fight of King Indra and Vritrasura was a magnificent fight of vibrations, energy oscillations and concentrated projection of thoughts in one unified direction.

Would it be possible today to use modern technology to project the power of thoughts to make inorganic materials, objects and consciousness of others to behave in the desired manner?

It was almost midnight, her mother was fast asleep. Ankita lay beside her and closed her eyes with one simple thought.

A wrong pronunciation changed the life of King Indra. Can sound create or destroy?

She decided to have a discussion with Dr. Jatin in the college tomorrow.

15.

Dr Jatin, who was seated on a side chair with his back to the computer, grinned after listening to Ankita's question.

'You are already much ahead on the subject, but for the sake of clarification and discussion, we will look at the basics and their applications.'

'Does there exist a weapon that can fire a directed wave of sound?' Ankita's question was specific.

'Specifically, no. Till date no sonic gun has been invented, primarily because sound deflects and expands in all directions while travelling in any medium. It is not possible to get it concentrated like a laser beam.'

'Can sound in metal be transferred to another medium by contact of surfaces? Let's say, can metal touching a body damage a living organism?'

Dr. Jatin turned his head towards her, giving her his full attention. 'What is on your mind exactly?'

Ankita explained the story of Vritrasura, King Indra, Rishi Dadhichi, his 'Vajra', nature forces and cause of sounds.

Dr. Jatin always knew that ancient sciences needed more research and attention than was being given by modern researchers. He almost jumped from his chair, "Are you trying to compare the story to a sonic gun?"

'Not exactly, but I have a research facility at home with a large collection of books.'

For the first time, Dr. Jatin realised why she was always found lost in her own world, her head burrowed in some book in the college. 'I will help you in the best possible way, Ankita.'

'I need some help in solving one riddle: in order to direct a sound beam of any frequency, the speaker has to be larger than the wavelength, as sound travels at 333 metres per second in the air, and that means that a one metre diameter speaker is needed to direct a sound of 333 Hz; achieving a directed sound with speakers smaller than this wave length is difficult.'

'I know Ankita, it doesn't sound feasible at the moment.'

'At the moment, why? You mean, Sir, is it possible that it can be changed some day?'

'Ankita, any branch of science has immense possibilities to explore, experiment and invent. There is always a possibility. If it is not there, it doesn't mean that it can never happen in the future.'

'But Sir, ultrasonic sounds can shatter thin glasses, it can pulverize a target.'

'And the person carrying the machine will get liquefied while firing the machine. First of all, how will one be able to carry the immense source of instant power?' Dr. Jatin took a deep breath. It was so difficult to answer all the questions raised by this brilliant girl. However, he enjoyed their discussion.

'You know Ankita, to create a 10-12 psi pressure that generates sounds of more than 130 dB exceeding the human hearing limit will require thousands of watts. How will you generate it for your experiments without government aided research? Secondly, even if an ultrasonic transducer is built for your experiment, to achieve destructive resonance, many megawatts of power are required.'

Ankita was surprised with the relevance of the story to the words of her professor.

'You know Sir, King Indra Dev is considered the personification of rains, clouds, lightning and thunder. Now I understand how he got the power to challenge the sounds of destruction created by Vritrasura. He was able to generate millions of megawatts of electric power in the clouds to fight the great Asura.'

Dr. Jatin started laughing, 'You are sharp and beyond my expectations. How cleverly you have been able to relate my words to your part of the research!'

'I come to your specific question. You know, Ankita, no living organisms, plants or animals have a common frequency. Each body part vibrates at a different frequency than the other. Like a moving car, engine, dynamo, AC pump, self-starter, cooling fan or even ruffling air on the body, they all have different frequencies of vibrations in a single car. That is also true for our bodies, our minds and our thoughts. The thoughts of happiness are in a different resonance of frequencies than thoughts of sad moments.'

He continued, 'Each of our body parts resonate differently, as blood travels in the veins, it creates a ruffling sound due to friction on the vein's surface. If you amplify and listen, you will find that the sound of the leg is different from that of the arms, the sound of the mind is different from that of the neck and the sound of the heart is different than that of the lungs.'

'Even to replicate the experiment of ancient times by modern ultrasonic transducers at a frequency of more than 20,000 Hz, you will need many secondary transducers to generate the desired frequency, with unlimited power backup. That your machine doesn't melt during such heat dissipation will again be a major area of concern. There's even a risk to your life during the experiment.'

'It was a fight between gods and demons. Even with the best modern machines, use and control of nature's forces cannot be replicated at least for now, with the present level of scientific knowledge.' Dr. Jatin looked at Ankita with amusement. Rarely did he get an opportunity to have a discussion with such a curious student.

'Any success reported on the infrasound?' Ankita asked her last question. She knew she was getting late and it was time to go home. She would continue the discussion with her supportive professor some other day. She picked up her bag and stood up, asking her question in a soft voice.

'No success recorded and I have not come across any research till date, but keep looking and you will find a way and an answer. Just keep moving forward.' Dr. Jatin packed up and came out with Ankita.

Ankita took the office key from his hand and locked the door, handing back the key once again.

She bid him goodbye and marched home. A few students were in the campus, it had a deserted look, players were shouting in the deserted playground.

16.

Nandkishor, his wife, daughter, Suresh Kumar, Rajpal and his wife started the journey to their ancestral village Mewla Gopalgarh at 9:10 p.m. after dinner. The programme was already late by two hours. However, the road was an expressway for most part of the travel and then passed through small stretches near the villages.

Rajpal's Maruti Eeco, his bread and butter, the 'Noida Express', started the journey.

Somehow, there was heavy traffic while coming out of Noida that day, delaying them further. Around 10:05 p.m., the vehicle climbed on the ramp of the expressway.

'Noida Express' was running as fast as it could. Rajpal, an experienced driver, was able to reach the left turn, only to land behind a long line of trucks.

They were already late and were getting delayed further. It was twelve past midnight when the Eeco was finally on the last lap of the journey. It moved on a lonely road for the remaining thirty kilometres. No traffic was seen after midnight on that road. Everyone was a little eager and desperate to reach home and were falling asleep in the vehicle.

The vehicle reached Palwal-Aligarh road and took a left turn to Hamirpur.

After two kilometres, Rajpal sensed that there was some sound of a batten stuck to the rear tyre and realised immediately that there was a puncture.

Everyone in the vehicle woke up.

Rajpal got down from the vehicle to check the tyres and with him went Nandkishor and Suresh Kumar.

Three persons were waiting for them just five meters behind. They jumped out of the bushes brandishing pistols. Nandkishor saw two pistols being pointed towards them. All of them were caught unawares but sensed the danger. It was too late, very late; the gang had trapped, ravaged and destroyed three families.

17.

Manju woke up as usual around seven in the morning and sat in the balcony, with the newspaper and a cup of tea.

On the front page at the bottom was a story of gang rape of two women and one girl, murder of two men and injuries to the third one. Police reached the scene because of a mobile call by a survivor to his relatives. The crime had happened after one o'clock in the night near Jewar. There was no patrolling police vehicle in the area that night.

The detailed news was also on the second page of the newspaper: 'Last night, six family members of a food vendor, an electrician and a driver travelling in a Maruti Eeco were trapped by a gang on Jewar-Mewla Gopalgarh road. One of the families, accompanied by the driver and his wife who were also neighbours, was going to attend a marriage function.

The criminals took the families hostage at gunpoint and the victims were pushed to the ground. Nandkishor and Suresh were shot dead while his wife, daughter and Rajpal's wife were allegedly sexually assaulted.

The gang also looted Rupees Two Lakh in cash and gift items, police said quoting the survivor, driver Rajpal, injured and shifted to the district hospital.

The driver narrated that when Nandkishor tried to resist, he was the first to be shot dead. Suresh Kumar, an electrician from the same village, tried to escape and another bullet hit him in the chest. The young man died on the spot.

The driver was severely beaten up as his wife begged them to have mercy on the women and the minor girl and said, 'We begged them to take the cash and gift items, but one young member in the gang was very aggressive and started abusing. He fired first without listening to Nandkishor.'

Rohit Srivastava, IG Police, Meerut Range, informed the media that the police had formed several teams and roped in the special operations group, surveillance cell, anti-extortion cell, crime branch, STF and teams from Aligarh and Bulandshahar to trace the criminals. He stated that the police have registered a case of murder, gang rape and robbery. Five expert teams of the crime branch had been constituted to take up the case on a war footing. Based on the descriptions given by the driver and the women, the three criminals had been identified as Bhure Lal, Manoj Kumar and Mukesh Kumar. They had been named in several other cases.

Manju tried to ignore the news, but it was one part of the news that attracted her, the name of the village Mewla Gopalgarh near Jewar and the name of one of the victims.

Perhaps she knew who Nandkishor was.

Her grandmother belonged to this village. She had been there several times in her early childhood and many images of the village flashed in her mind.

She read the full coverage again; there was no trace of the criminals, almost like a clean slate. Police could not find much relevant information.

Somewhere, from the shadows, Sumit Bhatnagar appeared, he was the criminal advocate for Bhure Lal, his grateful client. He was ready to fight the case in court and was prepared for any eventuality and would assist the police in the days to come.

He could be contacted in Lucknow.

18.

Bholaram Yadav informed Surender Nagar about the incident. The morning report with all details had been telecast to Lucknow at nine in the morning. Hem Pratap Singh, the Chief Minister came to know about the incident. The failing law and order situation was a burning issue in the newspapers.

Ved Prakash Dagar, DGP spoke directly to Surender Nagar for a few minutes due to his past connections and loyalty to the Chief Minister.

The DGP scratched his head in worry. The incident had taken a turn now as there was a rally of the opposition party in Lucknow, there was going to be a lot of clamour in the media.

19.

Ankita woke up and found her mother a little disturbed. She pointed out the news but Ankita could not understand.

Manju was a little tensed. 'You know, my grandmother belonged to this village. I have visited this village several times in my childhood.'

The incident disturbed Manju somehow but Ankita was unable to understand and say anything. It was bad news anyway and now there was some connection to some village.

'Mother, Papa will be returning tonight', Ankita changed the topic.

'Yes, make another cup of tea'. Manju left the newspaper.

It was yoga and meditation time after which she'd read mantras from 'Mantra Pushpa' for another hour before leaving for college. One video of an experiment of levitating little thermocol balls on the sounds created by two vertically opposite speakers caught her attention. She found it quite amusing that gravity could be controlled by sound. Did oscillations perform the levitation or gravity itself was an oscillation?

She did further research online. The words of Dr. Jatin were true, the internet was flooded with the same information and she stumbled upon some other facts.

Acoustic devices follow the inverse square law, which predicts the loss of sound at the rate of 6 to 8 dB (decibels) for each doubling of distance from the source, solely due to geometric spreading. The larger the diameter of a speaker; the higher and more effective was the frequency.

However, it did not fit in to her ideas of experiments. She needed some help on infrasonic devices, but not much relevant study material was available.

She again started reading one of the war stories and on the use of mantra with slow chanting, reciting them while launching weapons and harvesting the energy of mind. It all seemed fictional and mythological. She had seen it many a times in TV serials, where characters were reciting mantras while keeping an arrow on the bow and then there were special effects.

She kept on reading. Brahmastra was a severe weapon, almost like a modern fusion atomic bomb, but controlled by mind. The mind cannot control without vibrations, which is why the heat of radiation emanating from the Brahmastra launched by Ashwatthama in the Mahabharata war was countered by Arjun aaccording to the advice of Lord Krishna.

So, countering a nuclear weapon was a possibility as was a 'Shabda-vedhi bana', an arrow following the sound of the enemy.

It meant that the arrow heard and understood the sound made by the enemy and followed it in all directions, and kept following until it attacked. All guided with the power of mind, simple arrows but with terrific powers in comparison to the present science of satellite navigated missile. No answer, no research or no evidence was available now. All hidden somewhere, burnt down by invaders or lying in the deep bowels of the earth in stone boxes.

Lord Balaram chanted a mantra and blades of grass became real blades, hurling their fury on the Yadavas at Prabhas Kshetra, by the Arabian Sea in Veraval.

Humans are 'electrical' beings. They emit a range of electromagnetic radiations and mechanical vibrations. Frequencies of less than 7 Hz create positive vibes in the body with the most benefits and the worst frequency being 6.8 Hz.

Ancient people knew the use of a wide range of frequencies from chanting of mantras for healing to fighting wars with demons that had tremendous powers.

Mantras start a vibration that corresponds to a specific frequency, helping or overriding the desired effect. After a length of time, which varies among individuals, a mantra could vibrate organisms in tune with the natural frequency.

Infrasonic was a possibility. Dr. Jatin had a doctorate in modern physics, with awarded research on radiation emitted by moving sub atomic particles. He might be of help as he was her best friend and mentor, and was ever ready for a discussion.

She hurriedly left for college after a quick breakfast and getting a few reminders from her mother.

20.

Sumit Bhatnagar had passed his masters in law from Agra University. He was a man of varied interests. During his initial years of law practice, he used to fight criminal cases, but the cases lasted many years. The fee used to be paid very late or sometimes never paid at all. At one point of time, he decided to leave law practice and venture into some other profession.

Sumit worked hard, toiled day and night, however his humble background and need for money propelled him to look for new avenues.

It was then that he met Mithilesh Mishra, the chief of the emerging political party. Those were the rising years for the party. The party workers used to be caught repeatedly during party protests. A number of workers used to ransack public property during protests, even steal the PWD roadside items, cars, scooters and even escape with money bags.

Once caught by police, they needed some lawyer's help in getting away with the minor crimes. Settlement with the police was a major hassle and Mithilesh Mishra entrusted this work of protecting party workers to Sumit.

He was kept on the payroll of the party and became an important functionary of the political team, always working in the background.

With time, Sumit evolved as a criminal lawyer, sharp and reliable. He was ready to use every trick and loophole, in helping them to escape the law. The fee he earned now was many times more than that of other lawyers who were handling criminal cases.

He met Bhure Lal in his early days of infamy, for a paltry crime and got his case dropped easily with a warning. Bhure never looked back after that incident. He advanced in crimes and his lawyer, Sumit, in his fees.

He still remembered one incident in which one of the criminals he was fighting for in the court case went against him and started hunting him.

Bhure got into the picture. One day while returning from court with Bhure, he miraculously escaped the bullet fired at him, but the person behind it could not escape the reverse fire by Bhure. They ran out of the premises before any one got a clue. Sumit's attacker, collapsed there itself, and the police never came to know the truth and the case was still lying open.

Sumit did not forget Bhure since then. His whereabouts were not known to him, but he remained grateful to him for saving his life. When he read the news with the name of Bhure Lal in it, he knew that someone from Lucknow would contact him for repayment of debts that Bhure owed to the one sitting in power.

21.

Manju heard a voice. Someone was calling her and she tried to recognise the voice.

Her naani was calling her to the village but she did not want to return home. Her naani had not given her the permission to go alone to the marriage function nearby.

Naani wanted to accompany her lovely, seven-year-old grandchild, to introduce her to all her friends in the village. Manju wanted to play and go to the function immediately. She was angry. It was getting late, as the sound of the music orchestra at the function kept beckoning her.

Crying, in her blue frock, she ran to the nearby pond and climbed the tree that was leaning towards the village pond to get a better view.

Within a minute, she realised the danger ahead. She could not get down and the branch was slipping away from her hands.

'Naani, help me.' She shouted.

No one heard her and fear gripped the little girl. Panicked and aching, her little hands slipped from the tree branch. While falling into the pond, she had a fleeting glimpse of a boy running towards her, shouting for help.

The boy jumped into the pond immediately, it was deep for him near the tree but he had learnt swimming in this very pond.

The boy was able to hold the girl and bring her out of the water. By then, two other people had also reached there. Little Manju was crying in fear.

One man lifted her and ran to her naani's house.

Her naani came to know of her escapade andshe heaved a sigh of relief on seeing her. She spoke to the little boy with gratitude and admiration.

Naani knew the boy. 'Nandkishor you have saved my granddaughter, what would I have told my daughter. That I could not take care of her daughter even for a few days?

Nandkishor stood silent. He was a small boy and used to support his father at his chaat thela, a street food rickshaw. Going from street to street while pushing the cart; with not much business except at fairs and weddings. Their family survived with great difficulty in the village.

Manju never visited the village again and so, never met the boy again, but she remembered the name Nandkishor, the name of that village and her drowning incident. Her mother had told her the story of the boy who saved her life at the village pond many a times.

It was a long time ago.

Perhaps he was the same Nandkishor in the newspaper. The boy who had saved her life, was murdered that night and his entire family faced the trauma of that crime.

Manju sensed the connection between her and the newspaper story. Why was the name disturbing her?

Her eyes opened from the dream. It was early, four o'clock in the morning and Santosh was still sleeping. She decided not to disturb anybody.

She made a cup of tea for herself and sat in the drawing room.

Could she still help the family in distress?

In the morning Manju told Santosh about it and he was a little apprehensive of the whole situation. After all, it had been many years and with Nandkishor gone, who would recognise her.

Santosh advised Manju to forget the matter, and not to discuss it further with Ankita or anybody else.

Manju didn't know what propelled her curiosity, maybe a feeling of compassion. Destiny being what it is, she decided to meet the family someday.

It never occurred to her that the victims could be under police protection and they'd keep an eye on who was visiting the family. The Chief Minister was worried and so were the DGP, IG Police and DSP of the city and down the line, even Inspector Surender Nagar. Staff in civil dress, were supposed to submit detailed reports of all the persons, media, journalists, relatives and strangers meeting them or who were trying to meet them. Daily reports were being submitted to IG Meerut Range by none other than Inspector Surender Nagar and Sub-Inspector Bholaram Yadav.

22.

Ankita wondered about the slow speed of sound in the air and whether steel could be used to amplify the impact. If the change of medium was changing the speed of sound, was it possible to translate its impact on objects. Was this concept known to all the mythological characters she had been reading about all these years? There was no answer, and if modern science was unable to answer, why not mix them with knowledge in mythologies?

Santosh knew about the interests of his brilliant daughter. He was a busy person, but always appreciative of her. It was with his support that Ankita had been able to collect the literature since her high school days, reading and imbibing the basic principles. Several yoga courses had also helped her.

Ankita qualified for some of the well-known competitive exams easily and could have pursued graduation from any IIT, but she decided to stay in Noida and join the Government College to help her mother in the daily chores. Manju had been furious when Ankita had forgone her rank in IIT-JEE.

It had taken Santosh several days to convince Manju that if Ankita can qualify for one competition then she can clear the others in future, and even if not, there was nothing wrong in studying in Noida. After all, the books and syllabus remain the same, it was just a change in buildings and management cannot make such a huge difference.

Manju became fonder of her daughter as Ankita became more inquisitive about her passion for reading ancient literature on sounds, oscillations and vibrations. She compromised on everything else for the free time she needed to pursue her passion rather than follow the rigorous routine of being in the herd.

23.

It was a routine affair for the family to go on outstation visits once a year. Santosh and Ankita loved visiting places. Manju followed them with difficulty due to her frail figure but never escaped an opportunity to travel.

Where to go was the topic of a heated discussion between the three.

Ankita came up with the idea of going to Dholavira in Kutch during summer.

Manju laughed and her father smiled and asked, "Do you want to torture your mother?"

'No, papa, it will not be so hot in the mornings and evenings and if we go in an air-conditioned car to Dholavira then we will not have any problems. We will have everything planned, from our stay in Bhuj to our return. We will see the ruins before noon and depart in the night. You will like it, amazing phase of our civilization and history.'

'Yes, history of ancient India with which you are engrossed in all the time. There cannot be a better place, perhaps one of the remotest parts of Harappan civilization.' Santosh looked at Manju.

For the first time, rather than going to a hill station, the family decided to tour Dholavira in Kutch under the scorching summer Sun.

Ankita smiled. 'Don't worry mom, I am here.'

Manju smiled back at her. She was always happy in her daughter's company, nothing else mattered.

24.

Why did Ankita choose Dholavira of all places?

She thought that she would be able to trace resonance of uncommon sounds there in the dark of night.

The family travelled by train and reached Bhuj. It was a hot day. They decided to stay there for the night and journey tomorrow.

'So, what is the plan now?' Santosh asked before settling down for the night in Bhuj.

'I want to stay at the Dholavira Toran Tourist Complex for one night and will then go ahead as you desire.' Ankita responded.

'We can go to Veraval and Dwarka while returning to Delhi. After all, we have six more days' leave with us.' Manju was now determined to make the most of this trip in spite of the hot weather.

Nandkishor's name came to her mind from somewhere before she went to sleep.

She would visit the family some day after returning from the tour, Manju assured herself and fell asleep.

Dholavira was 230 kilometres away from Bhuj and it took four to five hours to reach by road, passing through Bhachau and then taking the left turn to Rapar. The great Rann of Kutch provides a majestic view on both sides.

The journey started after breakfast the next day in an Innova at 9:30 a.m. Manju, who had been least interested in seeing the area initially, was now most excited to see one of the remotest corners of the country. Everything was well planned. The outside heat did not matter, after all her husband had arranged for their stay and journey very well.

The family reached Toran Tourist Complex owned by Gujarat Tourism, which is a kilometre before the ruins, by seven o'clock in the evening.

All the three of them rested for some time after dinner and deliberated on the future course of action. Manju decided to take rest and Santosh with Ankita would go for an experiment in the silence of the dark night.

Ankita had brought two suitcases full of sound recording equipment of variable frequencies, oscillators, two laptops, amplifiers and many connecting cables with her luggage.

Her father had always been a curious and wonderful person, but a man with many passions. He always felt happy about the intuitive temperament of his daughter since her childhood. The father-daughter duo had a different world view and liked participating in intuitive experiments together.

It was around ten o'clock in the night when both of them got ready with all the testing gadgets brought from Noida. The suitcases were loaded in the Innova and they started on the road leading away from the ruins to a remote corner.

It was dark, there was no sign of any animal, man and almost no sound. After reaching a stretch of barren plain land, they stepped down and began opening the suitcases.

'What is the plan, Ankita?' Santosh again asked with curiosity.

'Nothing special papa. I will explain. I want to record the sounds at all the available range of frequencies and then project them on the modified oscillator at home. I want to study the inaudible sound ranges present here and their effect on objects.' Ankita was vibrant with excitement.

'Ok, let us start,' Santosh did not enquire further. He wanted to sleep after this experiment. It had been a long day of driving on empty roads.

Ankita started the receiver and connected it to her laptop. Her modified receiver was able to record all audible and inaudible frequencies. The circle on her laptop started moving slowly and in the lower corner table was a chart showing the frequencies of modulations ranging in thousands of divisions of one Hz to thousand Hz. The dish antenna installed on the tripod worked silently for almost two hours.

Everything went peacefully, except the two eyes that were watching them with awe and curiosity. Wearing vermilion clothes, he was going towards his hut in this remote part of Kutch. Very few ever saw him. There was a murmur in the village that a monk had been searching for the secrets of Dholavira for a long time. He was meditating most of the time or was busy with his computer.

Both were shocked for a moment. They never expected that they would ever find a monk at such an isolated place, in the heat of Kutch.

The monk smiled and said, "Ankita, I would like to meet you tomorrow. The answer to your research has a link here. You have to use your intuition cautiously and I hope you will never let anybody know the secret."

As he walked away slowly, both were shocked by the unexpected visitor.

Sleep had vanished from the eyes of Ankita and Santosh. Santosh started laughing at the monk's visit and they started winding up. Within half an hour, they reached the guesthouse.

After trying to sleep for some time, Ankita's eyes finally closed out of tiredness. She thought of having a discussion with her parents tomorrow.

25.

Manju was quite sceptical. 'How did he know the name of my daughter?'

'Maybe he listened to our conversation for quite some time, nothing much to worry about, it is a normal affair. Monks prefer isolation and like to meditate in remote places. The external environment does not bother them much. Let us get ready; we have to visit the main sites early in the morning and take rest at noon so that we are able to reach Bhuj by evening. In the night, we will move to Veraval by the Volvo sleeper coach. Has Ankita woken up?' Santosh was smiling.

Much to Ankita's bewilderment, no one discussed the incident of meeting the monk at night. She also decided not to remind them. The family got ready to visit the main Dholavira site and the ruins of the Harappan Civilization.

A local boy was eager to explain the history of the place and act as their guide. Santosh agreed to his charges and the boy was very happy to have them as his first customers. Then they saw one more family that they had met last night at Toran Guest House. It was quite a group now.

The ruins of the Harappan civilization lay in front of them, all the three started walking around the area.

Walking slowly, the group reached the dockyard site. A huge water tank was lying in front of them.

Their local guide spotted someone standing there. He was the same monk again in a light-coloured vermillion robe loosely hanging around his body.

'Swamiji, you came so early today.' The young boy seemed to be familiar with him. The monk smiled and answered, 'Waiting for all of them here.'

'Swamiji, you just frightened us for a moment last night,' Santosh was sarcastic.

'My name is Shivanand. Santosh, you can call me by name.' He was smiling, and had a bright face with glittering eyes. He looked different from any other monk Ankita had ever met.

Another person, who had also come to the Toran Guest House last evening, was Professor Dr. Mrinal Pandey, from IIT, Gandhinagar who recognised him. He had seen him participating in some of the discourses in Shiva Ashram many a time. The ashram was situated almost thirty kilometres away from Gondal, a small town near Rajkot. Locals knew him. He was a silent monk and very interested in the education of local children.

'He is a PhD in Physics with research on theory of vibration of atoms, and a renowned name because of his lectures on spiritualism. Every year he takes one week's leave from normal life and meditates in remote places. Lucky to see you here and I am surprised. His work is well-known the world over', the Professor introduced the monk to Santosh Sharma and he was bubbling with surprise and joy at meeting Swami Shivanand.

'So, Ankita what are your findings on sound?' Swami Shivanand changed the topic.

'Well, not finding the way to project sound energy on objects enough to move them. It was not just the Vajra wielded by King Indra that killed Vritrasura; there were effects of some sound energy also.' Ankita directly came to the point.

The monk started smiling. 'Your daughter is exceptional; she will find her way one day.'

Then he turned towards Ankita. 'Perhaps you will find the answer in Veraval. Just listen carefully by the side of the Somanath temple. Sounds of destruction and the words of Lord Balaram and Sri

Krishna are still navigating in the oscillations of the Arabian Sea's waves and air. They come from the ionosphere of mother earth. Practice the sound of AUM and meditate. You will find a relation of your observations there in the experiments in Prabhas Kshetra. I repeat Ankita, tread with caution. Sound is the genesis of the universe and cause of its destruction.'

'Thanks Swamiji, I shall be careful,' she said, bewitched by the happenings around her. It was the least expected piece of advice from an unknown person in one of the remotest places in India.

'Swamiji, when are you going back?' The guide interrupted.

'Two days from now, my son. On Dr. Pandey's special request, I have agreed to a brief meeting at the guest house in the evening. I hope Santosh you will join us.' Yogi Shivanand walked away slowly in the background.

To Santosh's surprise, familiarity between the monk and the Professor and guide melted away all doubts and ill-will towards him that had cropped up due to last night's incident. It was now a normal and usual meeting that could have happened at any moment, at any place.

Manju also ignored the whole affair and started enjoying the scenic sites. In spite of the hot weather, she wanted to make it a memorable trip. She knew very well, coming here from Noida was a lifetime experience. She could go to famous places any time and repeat it several times but this was going to be a unique journey.

Ankita imagined that perhaps she was close to an answer that she had been searching for so long. She had to analyse data, connect it with all the equipment in her mini lab and search for a solution to her quest.

Manju brought out the Canon DSLR camera from her purse, and handed it to Ankita.

Now it had become a photography session with all members for the next two hours where everyone was laughing, all the while wanting to leave the ruins at the earliest due to the rise in temperature.

26.

Swami Shivanand, with one of his disciples, reached Toran Guest house at five o'clock in the evening. The guesthouse manager arranged a round chair conference for ten people. They knew Dr. Mrinal Pandey, as he had come many times in the past on official visits with archaeological teams, state explorations and even with foreign university delegates. His love for Kutch was well known in the high circles of Gujarat Government, and they consulted him on matters related to Dholavira and the surrounding area.

Swami Shivanand started the conversation with them, asking about families, life and general discussions.

'As you are now aware, I am a doctorate in Physics and a monk by way of life. I come here every year to be in seclusion and pin drop silence in the nights. This place was part of a great civilization and reminds me of our great heritage.'

'I was very much surprised by the sight of some odd experiments being done by you in the night. No one dares to come out of the complex due to fear of wild animals and the silence here is more fearful. I really appreciate your courage and inquisitive nature to come out in the night and experiment.' Swami Shivanand was full of praise. He knew it was a rare event even for him.

He continued. 'I have been visiting this place for the last fifteen years. I have a small permanent hut here. In fact one of my disciples is always here, as young disciples come here for meditation and pass time in isolation, away from the crowd and hectic schedule in my ashram.'

Manju interrupted, 'It is so hot here in the day that it must be a torture to live here.'

'We are modern monks; we believe in science and engineering.' He laughed for a moment as he continued. 'The hut is well equipped with all modern facilities including air conditioning, and the state government has provided necessary electricity and water connections, with proper road and communication facilities. You are welcome any time; it is not far from here. How will you look for inner peace and conscience while keeping your body in distress? During each cycle of development, the best of science has helped us, why not now? And even today, we are interested in understanding the science behind their thoughts and inventions.' He looked at Ankita with curiosity.

'My daughter, what made you conduct experiments in the dark night, after coming to such a far-off place from your city?' the Swami turned his attention towards Ankita.

Ankita was hesitant for a moment and then after seeing the support of her father in his eyes, she explained the experiment, capturing even the inaudible sounds, resonance and modifying the same impact on objects, infrasonic assessment and its failure versus ultrasonic frequencies, Shabda-vedhi arrows and chanting of mantras beforehand by warriors.

Swami Shivanand listened to her with rapt attention. He understood that it was not a simple case, the girl was determined. However, what led her to research in this direction, what were the causes?

'Ankita, sometimes the answer lies in the source itself. We keep looking for them in the outside world. I hope you will find an answer to all your questions. I visit Delhi and even Noida sometimes. I remember there is one invitation for my lecture on Raas Leela by Shri Krishna Ashram.'

'Yes, it is near our house,' Manju was quick to respond.

Santosh immediately grabbed the opportunity to invite him for light refreshments at his house during the Noida visit, whenever it took place.

Swami Shivanand smiled. In his eyes, meeting people always had some reason, the sum total of karmas and destiny. He always tried to help, it was his inherent nature and karmic duty.

27.

It was an overnight journey from Bhuj to Veraval in Saurashtra.

The Volvo sleeper coach dropped them at Veraval bus stand in the morning. All three of them were tired and wanted to rest for some time. The unexpected coincidence of meeting Swami Shivanand was still fresh in the minds of Ankita and Manju.

There was no hurry. After all, the tour programme involved rest, visiting Somanath and other nearby temples and then recording possible ranges of frequencies of sounds at the Arabian Sea shore adjacent to Lord Shiva's temple.

28.

Hem Pratap Singh, the CM and the party chief, Mithilesh Mishra were worried about the news of this gruesome crime as it started having political ramifications. The opposition party had dug out the whole story. There had been a large-scale outcry in the media when the murder of his key opponent in Hamirpur had taken place.

What bothered the Chief Minister was the involvement of Bhure Lal in the crime. He was the same Bhure Lal who had worked for him several times in Hamirpur, carrying out every instruction meticulously. Bhure Lal was part of his first political victory.

Mithilesh Mishra and Hem Pratap Singh left the DGP in the spacious CM's office and decided to have a discussion in one of the hidden small cabins inside the main office.

More than an hour passed with the DGP silently waiting for them sitting on the sofa set. The unfolding drama was big and serious. The DGP was a close aide of the Chief Minister. Ved Prakash Dagar was promoted out of a seniority list of nine superiors in waiting for the top post and always held the Chief Minister in high regard. Only the Chief Minister came out from the cabin and the discussion started.

'Now what?' There was excitement in his eyes.

'Sir, we will take up the case on a war footing,' the DGP replied promptly.

'They need your protection and safety, save them till the elections. After that, you can have a free run. I owe a debt to the gang from a long time ago. Let me repay it.' Hem Pratap Singh was a little soft, barely audible in his words.

The DGP was shocked for a moment, but he knew his boss, the Chief Minister never did anything without political mileage.

When and how to take advantage? There was a saying in his circles, that whenever anyone helped Hem Pratap Singh once, he never left any stone unturned to save their interests in the best possible manner; and he needed the support of all kinds of people, with no moral compunctions.

The Chief Minister was asking for time until elections, perhaps for some assignment and then free action.

Hem Pratap Singh knew very well whom he could trust in this assignment. He was waiting for Sumit Bhatnagar, the loyal party man, to provide help to these three people and save some time for reactions. Mithilesh Mishra was categorical, encounter by police was not a viable solution; opposition men could breach the jail and if left in the open they will be trapped for taking action against their own people.

Sumit Bhatnagar was arriving this afternoon in Lucknow.

29.

Ankita was sitting with her father at the rest house in Veraval. It was turning into a serious morning as the discussion from last night was carried forward, and they had been discussing quite late in the night and were still arguing.

The idea of recording sounds at Dholavira was fresh in her mind, she wanted to mix the recorded sounds and see the effect. Santosh was quite sceptical of the idea, but he was still always open to her wild ideas.

Santosh started the discussion. 'Let us go back to basics. Acoustics deal with the study of mechanical waves in gases, liquids, and solids including vibration, sound, ultrasound, and infrasound. An audio engineer can record, manipulate, mix and reproduce sound. And you want to mix them and do some experiments.' He continued, 'The basics will solve your problems. Let me finish. It is Sunday morning and what is the harm in teaching my daughter. Let me enjoy tutoring you at this age as I used to when you were young.'

Manju brought them breakfast. It was special today with Gujarati local dishes served by the rest house.

Santosh continued, 'Sound is an oscillation in pressure, stress, particle displacement and particle velocity. Sound is a stimulus and sound is a sensation, a source that creates vibrations in the surrounding medium.'

Ankita started enjoying the lesson as her father was in a good mood today. He was trying to recapitulate his own knowledge and recollecting his past days. He had been a brilliant student and physics had been his favourite subject.

Manju joined them and became a part of the ongoing discussion, 'I heard the scientist wanted to create a sound gun.'

Santosh smiled at her. 'And where would you like to use them, Manju?'

Manju thought for a second, as she had been caught unawares by the question. 'Hmmm...'

Santosh knew that she always felt agitated by news of crimes and criminals in the media. After all, she was the daughter of the retired District and Sessions Judge of Bulandshahar.

'So Ankita, the behaviour of sound propagation is generally affected by three things, a complex relationship between the density and pressure of the medium and motion of the medium and the source itself.'

Santosh kept explaining in a rhythm, even solving mathematical problems.

Ankita sighed. Such a long lecture from her father on basic knowledge was baffling... It had been a long time since he had been working and was not conversant with academics anymore. It was only because of personal interest that Santosh used to promote

Ankita in her quest for knowledge.

'There may be n number of never-ending experiments, and you may never reach the result, how much time can you really devote?' Santosh started laughing.

'Till you marry dear.' Manju, as always, was worried about her getting married, even here on this tour.

30.

Ankita was eager to start the experiment. She loaded all the gadgets, her laptop, its batteries, fully charged to last at least six hours, antenna, tripod stand, oscillator, eight microphones of varied sizes, variable frequency oscillator connecting eleven chords for laptop bridge and hard disk drives with hundred terabytes of memory, connected with a single USB port with five inlets, all packed in two suitcases.

They decided to attend the aarti and rituals peacefully and then visit the Somanath temple, sit on the benches in the temple and enjoy the view of the Arabian Sea.

By the time they had dinner at a nearby restaurant, it was nine o'clock. The devotees were slowly leaving the temple.

Their Innova slowly entered the small road leading to the Arabian Sea shore, where the Yadavas had once fought among themselves on Prabhas Kshetra, the same place where the small and tiny blades of grass once landed on them with a fury, killing the last ones left after the carnage.

The sea was shining with waves striking the shore in rhythm, making it a memorable scene for Manju and Santosh. Somanath temple looked majestic from the shore.

Ankita started unloading the materials for her pet project.

Santosh thought it best to not interfere with his daughter's work and decided to enjoy the time with Manju, until Ankita asked them to return to the guest house.

The experiment started, everything was arranged and functioning fine. Huge data with variable frequencies from inaudible range of less than 20 Hz to more than 20 kHz was being recorded in the hard disk drives at a fast speed.

Sitting with another laptop, Ankita tried to listen to the sound through earphones as was recorded in Dholavira. No effect was found for almost fifteen minutes. She tried to convert the inaudible range to audible by converting the medium of materials on the laptop—steel, water, air, wood and many more. There were many options available, including fire, with varied temperatures. Ankita just kept clicking on the options one by one. The moment she switched the medium to sound of waves from the sea, she heard a faint blast.

How had it merged with the sounds she had heard earlier?

Her laptop was recording the ranges with full capacity, with huge data being transferred to hard disks. After two hours, she decided to stop for the day and sat with her parents for some time before leaving.

The family reached the rest house and went to sleep.

31.

Manju closed her eyes; Santosh was already asleep. She also tried to sleep. Tomorrow they would visit Dwarka and leave for Noida. She began to feel homesick. She fell asleep after some time.

The family left for Dwarka, after attending the pooja and aarti rituals dedicated to Dwarkadhish. They boarded the train from Okhla Railway Station to New Delhi.

The journey back home started and everyone was happy.

After twenty-two hours, they reached Noida. Home sweet home. Manju Sharma was relieved and relaxed.

32.

Ankita thought for a moment. She had come across on the net that sound could kill people. Did some agencies have sonic weapons already?

Even 154 decibels are not enough to kill anyone, unless, perhaps, you were stuck with your head inside the source of sound for a prolonged period.

150 decibels are usually considered enough to burst your eardrums but the threshold for death is usually pegged at around 185-200 dB. A passenger car driving by at 25 feet is about 60 dB, being next to a jackhammer or lawn mower is around 100 dB, a chainsaw next to you is 120 dB. Generally, 150 dB (eardrum rupture) is only achieved if you stand really close to a jet aircraft during take-off or you're near a terrific blast.

If one wanted to kill somebody with a sonic weapon, there is not a whole lot of research on how one could go about doing it. The consensus is that a sound loud enough could cause air embolism in your lungs, which then travels to the heart and kills. Alternatively, lungs might simply burst from the increased air pressure. In some cases, where there is some kind of underlying physical weakness, loud sounds might cause a seizure or a heart attack.

Infrasound can cause the eyeballs to vibrate, making it very hard to see.

Making a sound loud enough to kill someone or even damage the surrounding objects was not her aim but the mythological stories used low volume vibrations in the forms of mantra and sounds to energise the weapons.

Ankita again pondered for a moment that the human ear naturally amplifies oral data for the frequency range used by the human voice.

A blast of 210 decibels or more affects the inner organs—the lungs —and could cause internal injury that could lead to death. A blast will affect the body, and would do so very violently.

Many weapons have been dreamed up by defence agencies, but they never actually built them.

Sonic weapons fall into two categories: those that involve audible frequencies, and those that are either ultrasonic or infrasonic and so are inaudible.

The effect of sound on humans is complex. It can vary depending on the frequency, modulation, loudness and time of exposure, environment, and the age and hearing characteristics of the individual.

There are two ways ultrasounds can harm humans. The first is that it can heat up cells in the body, causing damage. The second is that ultrasounds can cause 'cavitation'.

This happens in air as well when it travels through an object, such as the body. Cavitation is possible when the pressure difference between a strong push and a strong pull in a very loud sound causes bubbles formation.

Cavitation can by contrast, occur in the fluid of body tissues or cells. The extent of these biological effects depends on how the sound reaches the person being 'attacked'.

Ultrasound is directional and the precise alignment would be in millimetres that would be needed to hit someone at a distance.

Given that it is hard for powerful ultrasound to reach us, and most of it bounces right off our skin, it seems to be a strange choice of weapon. Ankita realised that warriors, rishis, devas and asuras used infrasonic sounds for all purposes.

Ankita was now worried on how to proceed further. She wanted to build a device that could catch natural vibrations of any object, catch the frequency, modulate and resonate, and amplify them many times and send it back in the desired vibrations of the varied frequencies. It was literally destroying the object with its very own natural frequency, a common term called modulated amplifications.

As to why she wanted to try it, she wasn't aware. The idea had come from reading scriptures and she was obsessed with the idea of battles with devas and asuras, kings and demons and the use of sound in those battles. The concept of the 'Shabda-vedhi bana' overtook her mind. To solve the puzzle of an arrow following sound took over her thoughts day and night.

Santosh was amused with her comically driven fancy world of sounds, mantras, weapons, wars, thunder, silent meditation and the modern way of understanding the same. His brilliant daughter and her wild ideas!

33.

One more week had passed, life had started coming back to normal after the long trip, and the thought of visiting Nandkishor's house started disturbing Manju again.

Finally, Manju decided to discuss it with Santosh in detail. It had been so many years, and she didn't remember the event too well. She had drowned in a village pond and a boy had saved her—these facts were known to Ankita and Santosh, but whether the boy was the same person who had been murdered that night was what evaded her.

Santosh also felt pity and sympathy for Nandkishor. He had always been grateful to the almighty for bestowing upon him such a considerate life partner and dedicated homemaker. She was intelligent and saved him from making erroneous decisions many a times, survived many a crisis and was always willing to help. Santosh had a high regard and sense of pride for his wife.

When Manju requested him to visit Nandkishor's home in Mamura, he agreed.

Santosh Sharma could never have imagined the ordeal of chain of events that such an insignificant decision as visiting Nandkishor's house would set in motion and change the future of their family, propelling them into a dangerous world of deceit, lies and death threats.

34.

Ved Prakash Dagar, the DGP was surprised. This time, the orders of the Chief Minister were explicit. In his entire career he had never seen any political boss issue directions through an unofficial order to protect criminals.

But what was their connection? His mind was reeling under tremendous pressure. He decided to invite Kulbhushan Verma, the Intelligence Chief to his office for a cup of tea.

'You see Kulbhushan, I am so surprised by the orders. There is more to the story that I am not getting, right?' The DGP went into a reflective mode.

Kulbhushan Verma decided not to react, he knew the story but silence was better than any explanation. Either way, one day they would be eliminated by their identities and not by the deeds.

'Who will take up the task of finding them within a week?' Kulbhushan countered with a question rather than by replying to Dagar's query.

'That can be taken care of, you just find the reasons.' The DGP looked straight into the eyes of the Intelligence Chief.

The hunt to know the whereabouts of Bhure Lal, Manoj Kumar and Mukesh Kumar was started by the police, with Rohit Srivastava, IG Police, Meerut range being in-charge of the operations.

Surprisingly, it was not the police, but Sumit Bhatnagar who succeeded, through a long series of phone calls day and night and feedback, over a week. He decided to inform Hem Pratap Singh personally and receive the action plan.

35.

Three months after the death of Nandkishor and Suresh Kumar and the gruesome incident, Manju left to meet the family in distress in Mamura. She hadn't in her wildest dreams imagined that the police had been conducting surveillance for the last three months by posting two constables in civil dress in the area near Nandkishor's house. The reports were being transmitted to IG Meerut Range weekly by Inspector Surender Nagar and his deputy Bholaram Yadav.

It was a precautionary measure to avoid any mistakes by the media and to protect the family caught at the centre of this widely reported case, to keep them away from the public gaze.

They had been able to crack some cases in the past, as criminals came searching for the victims' whereabouts, using strategy and connections. The cases were rare and it was a low probability psychological trap.

The car stopped near the congested lane leading to Nandkishor's house. Manju, wearing sunglasses and a saree, inquired about where the family lived. People had become familiar with the house as a number of reporters, local politicians and even one state Cabinet Minister had also ventured into the area. However, few visited the family now. It was old news now, with the fast-changing dynamics of crime news, the media was least interested in an old story.

Manju stopped for a moment in front of the door and rang the bell several times. A woman appeared, but she did not open the door and kept looking at her. Manju said she wanted to talk to her. The lady gave her another blank look. Finally, Manju took the name of the village and the name of her naani. The woman kept staring at her but asked, 'Are you Manju?'

'Yes,' Manju replied, a little surprised. The woman opened the door, and closed it as soon as Manju entered.

A camera looking straight at the door, recorded the incident.

36.

Manju was surprised that the family knew about her. Nandkishor had narrated the story of saving a girl in his village many years ago. When the family migrated to Noida, they were busy in making ends meet, they never really thought of looking for her. It was a forgone and lost history in everyone's life. Nandkishor's wife, Sujata and daughter Sakshi were looking at Manju in amazement. The misery written on their faces told the story of that night, the agony left to live out every day, every moment.

'Didi, we should have died that night. With Sakshi's father gone, we have been left to die every day and my daughter will not be able to live.' Tears rolled down Sujata's face.

Hundreds had visited them since the last three months—policemen, journalists, members of the media, social workers, but except for the talks, there was nothing. The sole earning member of the family was gone and Rahul Kumar was a broken young man.

He brought the 'Noida Express', Maruti Eeco back to Rajpal's home. Rajpal was unable to drive and had not been able to recover from injuries since the last three months. Several fractures including broken ribs and hip joints took many surgeries in the District Government Hospital of Noida. Rahul used to visit him regularly and failed to do any business now.

The family did not earn a single rupee and whatever little savings they had were coming to an end very fast and they were faced with destitution.

Manju felt paralysed; words were coming out with a lot of difficulty. The little girl's ravaged face and eyes were telling the story of hate, fear and agony of living life one more day. She had tried to commit suicide; Manju knew from the newspapers.

Sujata offered her tea. Manju tried to console Sujata, 'Don't hesitate to call me for any help and come to my house someday. I will try to find some way out to help, there is no point in returning to the village. I might have met you for the first time, but Sakshi is also my daughter. It is my duty to help you.'

Sakshi stared at her without uttering a single word. Very few had promised help. The family had no money left for paying rent or for kitchen expenses, and then there was the ordeal of police investigation.

Manju decided to leave the house after staying with them for forty minutes, unable to bear the agony and crisis. The report of her visit, with photographs and timing reached Surender Nagar and Bholaram Yadav.

Bholaram, after seeing her photographs, tried to remember, where had he seen her, but could not recall. Noida was not a small city, however something struck him and he asked for the details of the family from his area in-charge. He came to know that she was living near his government colony; perhaps he had seen her in some market or passing by on the roads.

Manju narrated the details of her visit to Santosh and Ankita. There was a lot of sympathy and curiosity.

Santosh extended financial help and advised Manju to give them twenty thousand rupees on her next visit.

37.

Bholaram was curious about the visit of an unknown woman to Nandkishor's family. Many relatives and others had visited the victims, he had been a part of the FIR proceedings and identification of criminals. Everything seemed to be normal, the case was peculiar in many ways, but for him, it was just one of many cases. During his twenty-two years of service he had witnessed many gruesome crimes. There was a meeting in Lucknow. His boss Surender Nagar had been called by the DGP for an important discussion.

The meeting began in a closed room with the Intelligence Chief also being present. There was no information about the whereabouts of the three according to the police. The Chief Minister was furious with the DGP.

The pace of events was getting faster, with the state elections just eight months ahead. Hem Pratap Singh, was in a hurry. He did not want the three persons to land in the hands of the opposition party.

After the meeting, he called Inspector Surender Nagar for a personal hearing. 'Keep in touch with Sumit Bhatnagar and take care of them.' The Chief Minister finally closed the meeting.

38.

Ankita was a little worried about her mother's unexpected concern for Nandkishor's family. However, after Manju's emotional appeal to help their family at this difficult time, she relented. She wished that her mother would close the chapter after giving financial help.

Manju again reached out to the family, this time her face was a little more familiar to Sujata and Sakshi. Rahul Kumar was in the village for some police work and to sign some papers. Life was difficult. When Manju offered the money to Sujata, tears started rolling down her cheeks.

'Didi, we will return the money back to you. He never accepted any help from anybody in his lifetime. He used to work day and night, but never went for any recommendations to anybody.' Sujata was helpless and Sakshi looked at Manju, then tears started rolling down her cheeks. Manju always felt agony on seeing her face. Sakshi was getting weaker with each passing day and refused to eat in spite of her brother's requests.

Manju returned from the visit. Near the society gate, there was a police surveillance Innova waiting for her, Bholaram got down and greeted Manju.

Manju was a little surprised, 'What has happened Inspector Sahib?'

'Nothing special, Ma'am. I just want to talk to you for a minute.' Bholaram was a little confused about how to take the conversation forward.

Manju replied, 'Why don't you come to our flat and have a cup of tea?' Bholaram immediately followed her.

Ankita opened the door, with a book in her hand. She could not understand the reason for the police officer's presence with Manju at their doorstep.

Anyway, Bholaram did not look bad. He was almost the same age as her father though he looked more like a teacher who had been given a police uniform by mistake.

Bholaram's questions were general in nature. The revelation of Santosh being an Under Secretary in the Ministry of Defence was enough for him to cut short his queries. Manju told him about the drowning incident in her native village and Nandkishor's connection and why she visited them, even telling him about extending financial help.

Nice family, Bholaram thought for a moment.

Ankita telephoned her father and told him about the courtesy visit to the family by Sub-Inspector Bholaram Yadav.

While picking up his cup of tea, his eyes caught some odd-looking electronics, sound forks, wire connected to speakers and some white coloured balls lying on the dining table.

'What do you do, Ankita?' Bholaram was curious. Both his sons were studying engineering. With time, he had become familiar with science.

Ankita eagerly replied, 'I am studying the impact of sound on objects. I will show you.' She was happy to show him her efforts.

'Ok, let me understand', teacup in hand, Bholaram looked a little amazed.

Ankita started the experiment. There were some thermocol balls hanging on almost invisible wires. She opened the laptop. The diagram opposite the balls was still. On the laptop screen, a line appeared like an ECG reading. Then the vertical bar started rolling, with a lot of vibrations appearing on the single line almost like a bell and then a point, again blank and again the same.

The cursor started crossing the vibrations. The moment it crossed the bell, the balls swung into action at once, striking back with sudden force.

What Bholaram heard was a creak and bang for almost five seconds.

He was amused and started laughing. 'Good, keep it up. This is like a magic show.'

Still laughing, Bholaram stood up, folded his hands in greeting and left.

39.

Today was Saturday and a holiday for Santosh. An old friend of his in Greater Noida had invited him a while ago for the birthday celebrations of his son. Santosh and Manju decided to attend the function and have lunch with them. Ankita said she was busy with college assignments and couldn't go with them.

In the evening, after lunch, Santosh and Manju left home in their car to their friend's house in Greater Noida. The road was clear, with less traffic.

There was a call for Bholaram from his son Shubham from Greater

Noida where he went for special classes on Saturdays. He wanted to return home from the Greater Noida Engineering College.

By coincidence, it was some official inquiry for which Bholaram had come to the DSP Greater Noida office. While returning in the evening, he decided to pick his son up on his way back home. Around five o'clock in the evening, he picked up his son from the roundabout and Shubham sat on the back seat, one constable by his side, the wireless radio was kept on. Some surveillance tips from the intelligence team was being discussed in a heated conversation.

The vehicle crossed the roundabout near Galgotia College and left for the under pass via the express way service lane.

There was a sudden burst of messages on the wireless intercom in the police vehicle. One Maruti Swift car had been intercepted near the underpass.

Bholaram, the constable and the driver became alert. The vehicle moved slowly towards the second roundabout. Bholaram's eyes widened as he saw the scene, sensing the danger ahead. The vehicle crossed the circle and moved towards the underpass, the left-hand turn was four hundred meters ahead.

All of a sudden four police vehicles appeared to be approaching the Maruti Swift. One from the wrong direction, another vehicle zoomed past the vehicle of Bholaram, one more gypsy again from the wrong direction from the service lane to expressway.

The stationary Swift restarted and took a U-turn and the police vehicle confronted the Swift. There was a shot fired and then one more shot from the other police vehicle.

Bholaram was now in the thick of action unexpectedly.

It was at the same time that Santosh and Manju reached behind Bholaram's Innova in their car and stopped behind it after seeing some problem. They were on their way home and were going to take the service lane to the expressway.

The Swift ran amok moving towards his vehicle, the constable drew his revolver and fired, one of the assailants fired back at them.

Another bullet shattered the front glass of Santosh's car and hit

Manju's seat who was sitting in the front.

Manju cried out loud, 'What happened?'

The Swift crossed the vehicle going full throttle. It crossed the circle within seconds and took the right turn and then the left.

Bholaram saw the smashing of the rear window glass of his Innova.

He ran towards it and opened the door.

There was blood on the seat. His son Shubham had died on the spot, hit by a bullet to his chest that was fired by the person on the left side of the door in the Swift, while crossing the Innova.

Santosh and Manju came down from the car and approached the police vehicle. They saw Sub inspector Bholaram standing still, panic written on his face.

It took Santosh and Manju five minutes to understand what had really happened. Bholaram was frozen and looked almost dead.

Manju realized that it was the same Sub-Inspector who had come to her flat yesterday, all smiling and laughing over a cup of tea.

In the meantime, all the three came down from the Swift and stopped near one of the society gates. They walked fast, and took another left turn.

An auto-rickshaw was moving in their direction. They stopped it and agreed to the amount the driver asked for. They took the second expressway cut, on the other side of the underpass, near the bus stand.

The auto rickshaw drove away and vanished from the scene.

The Swift was nowhere in the range, the intercom was shouting like hell, and all the other four police vehicles were in search of the Swift.

They found it empty with no one around it.

The auto rickshaw stopped near the bus stand. Luckily for the three, the bus to Botanical Garden arrived within seconds, and they boarded the bus.

News was out in the media and reached the public. There was an outcry, from Delhi to Lucknow, TV anchors shouting at full volume about the law and order situation in the state. It was a hoarse cry.

40.

Bholaram's family was shattered. The younger of the two sons was dead for no reason, for no fault and the police department was critical about using a government vehicle for personal errands.

What Bholaram was unable to comprehend the coincidence and the role of the culprits in the murder of his brilliant son. Was it because he was a part of the investigation in the Jewar case?

Bholaram's heart was filled with rage and vengeance. He should have shot all the three persons on the spot. However, they had vanished without a trace with no information from any source.

Bholaram's wife Sumita became mad, crying all the time as relatives and friends visited their house. From morning to night, he was in talks with friends and informers.

Santosh and Manju visited his house the next day, and sat silently. Bholaram knew the law, his department and their way of working. Except for encounters, any action by him would land him in jail.

In addition, he knew all too well that he would never be able to solve a 'why-problem' with a 'how-to problem'. Traditional ways of solving crimes were not going to help in this case anyway.

Shobhit, his elder son, came from Jaipur for the last rites and found his mother mad with grief and his father looking blank.

41.

It was a great day for Ankita. She was elated and surprised. Her experiment with copper lenses for projecting sound had gone extremely well. To her surprise, the change of medium from metal to air created a convergence of waves to a point and she was able to control or decide the diameter of projection on any object. The thermocol balls were now striking on the walls with ferocity.

The experiment was so powerful that she could make a small

whisper into a force of sound waves with almost a micro bomb like effect of small capacity. Such was the impact of waves that she was able to break glass with specified whole sizes, without leaving the whole glass broken. The range was active up to two hundred metres.

Ankita was now more engrossed in mythology, sounds and impact of these sounds in stories, hymns and verses. Reading story after story she was convinced that the biggest power the Devas used was conversion of sound into weapons against Asuras and that Asuras were not so proficient because it involved meditation and practice of silence and this was a weak point for the Asuras.

For Ankita it was fun time, light hearted as always and in the company of her passionate and loving parents as usual.

42.

She met Dr. Jatin after a long time. The moment she saw him, Ankita grabbed the opportunity to discuss the subject once again.

Dr. Jatin was free today, his classes had gotten over and there was no workload from the college side too.

Dr. Jatin informed his wife, that he might be late today, as he wanted to discuss some research work with Ankita. She was a known figure in his house also. He always gave her example to his children, the stories of leaving prestigious institutions for the sake of living with family, fascination with ancient sciences, sounds and what not. His children had even taken a picture with her and had it fixed on their drawing room wall.

Ankita had created this image through hard work and passion.

Finally, it was going to be a day of heated debate and discussions and both were ready with their armours.

'So, where had we left the discussion, Ankita?'

'Infrasonic sound gun.'

'I researched a lot and found something that might interest you.'

'By creating sound at a natural frequency, we can achieve the resonance of the materials to vibrate, and if sustained with enough energy, we can cause the material to break apart and disintegrate. Ankita, you will need a strong sound pressure wave to make this happen, so that resonance equals the amplitude of vibration to increase the vibrations of atoms to break them apart.'

'And Sir, this is not possible in a small lab.'

'So where are you focusing now?'

'I repeat, infrasonic sounds, like Shabda-vedhi arrow, listen to the sound and then follow it everywhere.'

'That is mythology, Ankita. Present science has no proof of it, even if it was possible once upon a time.'

Ankita paused for a moment and then told him about meeting Swami Shivanand, who had a PhD in Physics.

'Sir, tell me something about sounds with less than 20Hz frequency.'

'Surprisingly, elephants can hear 1 Hz to 2,00,000 Hz. Do you know that we are able to hear only 20 Hz to 20,000 Hz? Even dogs can hear 50 Hz to 45,000 Hz and cats even higher, up to 8500 Hz.'

'I know Sir. The ticking of the quartz watch is at 32 Hz, drizzle and light rain 13-25 Hz and mosquito sound at 17-20 kHz. The list is endless, people know it. I repeat for the sake of repetitions; the intensity of sound wave decreases with increasing distance from the source. It follows the inverse square law, a 60-dB sound at 1 m drops to 30 dB at 2 metres distance. The basics will lead to answers, yes, my father also says the same thing, that basics will lead me to the answer.'

'Our body can tolerate 85 dB of sound intensity for eight hours without any hearing damage, but raise the sound intensity and the time will reduce drastically, so even 7 Hz sound of very high intensity can damage the organs of a healthy person.'

'After reading all the literature, the science behind it and understanding all the stories, I know that sound is powerful. I have even heard that "Nada Brahma", a treatise by Lord Brahma says that this universe is a manifestation of sound. We are made of sound. Science today is trying to understand the difference between waves and particle theory, all its effects and even applying the uncertainty principle to these wave equations.'

The discussion began heating up with time.

'So, you are researching focussed sound effect on mind and bodies. May I know the reason?' Dr. Jatin was really baffled for a moment.

'I am trying to find out what our ancient sciences said about sound, why saying AUM is part of meditation, why the fight between Lord Indra and Vritrasura involved sound, why Lord Krishna and Balaram used sounds in the wars and how an arrow could follow a sound, how did it use the radar system created by the mind?'

'And even if you know, what will you do?' Dr Jatin laughed.

'I will experiment by capturing the natural frequency of objects and resonating them.'

'It can be dangerous, Ankita. You can be harmed.' Dr Jatin was shocked with the gravity of problems now. The simple dialogues did not remain so simple.

'Sir, I know that ultrasonic sounds of 2.5-4.0 KHz at 150 dB can create nausea, discomfort, disorientation, reduced sensory functions or severe pain. But how do I achieve the same result with infrasonic frequencies, because creating them will not need much power?' Ankita's question was specific.

'Killing without weapons. Perhaps if you are looking for solutions, you should become part of India's defence system. I can help you get a job in DRDO or even with the PMO.' Dr Jatin tried to amuse her. With her depth of knowledge, he could foresee that her research could be used for the nation.

'You know Ankita, use of infrasound can lead to imbalance, intolerable sensations, incapacitation, physical damage, body cavitation and even death by uncontrolled vibrations of organs in the body.'

Dr. Jatin continued, 'It is a fact that certain infrasonic frequencies can change algorithms of the brain and the nervous system and can cause fear and anger, thus affecting the heartbeat rate. Our internal organs such as the heart, liver, stomach and kidneys are attached to the bones by tissues and vibrate with low frequencies, around 12 Hz. Any attempt to resonate them with any external device will lead to permanent damage. Be careful, your research can land you in a dangerous situation.'

'I know Sir, but it can also help my country, with us taking a lead on many countries as well as countering the threat of many countries. I know the ramifications and the dangers.' Ankita was lost in her thoughts, gazing into the nowhere reflectively.

Today, as Dr. Jatin, understood the depth of her knowledge, he was awestruck for a moment.

'So finally, where have you reached?'

'It is in the heart where the answer lies. It is the most vibrant organ in the body after lungs.'

Dr. Jatin jumped from his chair. 'What did you just say?'

'Heart sounds are generated by the beating of the heart and flow of blood; sounds created by heart valves. You can listen to three unique sounds - lub, dub and silence or heart murmurs. These heart murmurs are created by the turbulent flow of blood based on pressure dominance in the valves. You have to understand the working of the heart. It is the answer, where the Shabda-vedhi bana or arrow follows and strikes.'

'How is that possible?' Dr. Jatin was lost in his thoughts.

'We have to understand the workings, whether its frequencies and the sounds it creates can be captured.' Ankita was looking him in the eye.

'Any radar can capture it.'

'As I see, the heart sound is captured at 46+-2Hz for a normal person, and can even go up to 70 Hz +-3 Hz for abnormal persons.'

'But that is a normal sound, not infrasonic sound that you are focussing on'. He replied armed with his knowledge from their discussions.

'I am focused on the nerves of muscles that the heart is hanging on, and it varies from person to person.' Ankita concluded with this reply.

Dr. Jatin knew that his student was much ahead in the experiments and research available presently.

His wife was calling. Dr. Jatin stopped for the day.

43.

Ankita Sharma packed her bags. She knew that she had to carry it alone. No help was available, no answer from the best of research of the world. She was much ahead of any university in the world even with their research facilities.

The audible range of sound of the first heartbeat was about 0.14 second, and the second beat about 0.11 second. To make any equipment capture it within the same lub-dub cycle, amplify it and revert with amplified resonance of such a powerful frequency as to disintegrate the atoms working in the heart itself was a comic idea. The muscles supporting the heart then vibrate with frequencies of 6 Hz to 12 Hz.

It was the concept behind the Brahmastra, it was the science behind the Pashupati-astra of Lord Shiva. Yes, sound was the science behind the art of warfare, the logic behind mantras being chanted by the Devas before shooting arrows, it will be the technology behind the missiles and future of wars.

She understood the concept from the mythologies of great wars of the kings and demons, from Devas and Asuras, from Mahabharat, from Ramayana, but what should she do now?

They had always known the science behind the sound, oscillations, modulated amplifications and the truth, the truth lost on the shores of time.

44.

Bholaram was a changed man now. Most of the time he just sat silently in the control room, listening to the conversations and orders. His junior staff was a little wary of the silence but understood the trauma being faced by him after his son's death.

He kept on thinking about his son, his fault for giving him a lift in his official vehicle, the three persons present in the Swift, his fate and destiny of being a police personnel.

There was something that his destiny, his karmas, his past life, his agony could not bear away. Who were the people in the Swift? Were they enemies from this life or a past life? Why was Shubham's father to witness this incident? The face of his son kept floating in front of his eyes on sleepless nights.

Why, after all, had this happened to him? If he was not at fault, then he had to take revenge in this life, but how?

As they killed without knowledge, without any planning, without any motive, with a weapon that was not intended for his son, he had to reply with their karmas in place.

Perhaps, Ankita might be able to help. He had a gut feeling, his sixth sense reminding him to find the remedy of agonies, the furies of his thoughts.

45.

Late in the evening, Manju received a call from Nandkishor's family. Sujata and her daughter Sakshi wanted to talk to her and come to their house.

She agreed and requested them to have dinner with the family. Sujata came and requested for some financial help to which Santosh and Manju agreed.

It was for the first time that Santosh and Ankita met the little girl who had survived rape and been witness to her father's murder. She understood the feelings of her mother, like her elder sister.

Sleep was nowhere in Manju's eyes that night. She would have killed everyone involved in the crime bare handed.

46.

In Shloka Society in Sector 51, Noida, barely a km away from Bholaram'shouse, a flat was hired by Sumit Bhatnagar. All the three fugitives - Bhure Lal, Manoj Kumar and Mukesh Kumar - were hiding there, daringly in the heart of the city without any fear.

At lunchtime, Sumita called Bholaram as she was feeling some discomfort in her chest. She was coming to terms with her son's death and trying to save her failing health. Her desire to eat had gone down drastically. She had not been keeping well. Bholaram took a half-day's leave to visit the doctor in Siddhartha Hospital, Sector - 132, Noida.

He reached the hospital in his personal car. While parking the car, he saw a man getting into a Honda Amaze.

He tried to remember where he had seen him. The Amaze drove away slowly and vanished from his sight. Bholaram was already late for the appointment and the doctor was ready to leave. He concentrated on the visit and started walking towards the OPD.

While waiting for his turn, Bholaram again tried to remember the face he had seen in the parking lot.

After the doctor's visit was over, he left his wife sitting in the car park and walked up to the parking lot manager at the exit gate. He was in police uniform, and the young boy decided to oblige him. He gave him the number of the Amaze, written in his diary. Bholaram came back to the car and drove home slowly.

He had seen the face somewhere. He wanted to see him again so that he could recollect. Without asking for any help from his subordinates, he decided to investigate the matter.

Ramesh Kumar had recently purchased the car and the address given was that of a rented apartment. He decided to go to the address. Three people were living there, and the flat had been hired a week before his son's murder in broad daylight.

47.

Bhure Lal and his team were ready for the next assignment, ever grateful to Sumit Bhatnagar and Hem Pratap Singh. They all knew that their prayers had been answered and they would live another day.

An unusual and peculiar situation, as each of them was trying to repay their debt of deeds to Bhure Lal.

He had been an accomplice in the political journey of Hem Pratap

Singh. At the beginning of his career, this one-time Bhure Lal had saved an attempt of murder by an opposition party shooter by moving around in his jeep in one of the villages of Hamirpur.

For Manoj Kumar, he was a financial benefactor. He had helped him in his wife's operation and even supported him during times of financial crisis.

Mukesh Kumar would have been jailed for his first offence had Bhure Lal not contacted the local SHO, who allowed him to escape. Caught again for stealing a motorcycle, the owner having caught him red handed, he escaped while being sent to judicial custody courtesy Bhure. Then a third time, while in a gun fight as he had tried to take away a steel loaded truck, Mukesh was hit with two bullets in his legs and was left to die on the road. Mukesh Kumar's last call to Bhure not only saved his life but also won unwavering loyalty from him.

Mukesh Kumar, the youngest of the three in the group graduated to become a hard-core criminal and the right hand of Bhure.

Then there was Sumit, he owed his life as well as profession to Bhure. From meeting the party chief to moving ahead with his law practice, being an average criminal lawyer to living a respectable life and escaping a shootout. He was indebted to Bhure on many fronts.

When Hem Pratap Singh came to know about the Jewar incident, he was very furious, Bhure and his team were not supposed to get involved in petty crimes. Somehow, they had gotten carried away under the influence of alcohol that night. Drinking since evening, Manoj wanted to do some mischief, anything. He could not control himself that day, and they had run out of money.

Sumit Bhatnagar somehow sensed that this time it was not going to be easy. Surender Nagar was loyal to the Chief Minister for his father's political connections, but not up to the mark while handling a sensitive case like this.

48.

Bholaram approached Santosh for a meeting and spoke to his family for half of the day, much to everyone's shock and bewilderment.

Santosh and Manju decided that they would never like to get involved in the issue. Helping Nandkishor financially was a separate matter and taking revenge for a crime was another. It was not their job to get involved in such matters.

Manju even tried to forget the daylight shooting. They could have been killed on that day. Life was always so full of surprises and they were ready for any exigencies, it was part of the nature and upbringing in the family.

Santosh was very clear in his head; he was a government servant. The chances of being killed on a safe footpath were equal, even worse than being killed in a war.

There was nothing to get personal about.

Santosh had already registered an FIR at the police station. He was well aware about the deteriorating law and order situation in the district, but things change with time and a million citizens were living in this thriving city.

The fear of death was absent from his mind, he was least concerned. He always used to tell stories of the young boys fighting at the borders, and he used to meet them during official field visits. He was not averse to his daughter joining any defence establishment, even as a scientist.

49.

Next week Bholaram focused his energies on the Amaze. He decided to keep a close watch on them. Usually, one person used to come out every day and he was not the same person each time, so his suspicions increased. Every time he remembered the faces, but his efforts did not yield any results and his gut kept telling him that there was some connection.

Suddenly, in the middle of the night Bholaram woke up and realised that perhaps he was the person sitting on the left side of the

Swift car, who had fired the bullet that killed his son.

Bholaram could not sleep the whole night. There was only one solution.

The next day, he and Ankita met to go for a morning walk to the nearby garden. He wanted the instrument he had seen while drinking his tea at her house. Ankita laughed and explained that it was her mind that orchestrated the whole experiment and amplified the oscillations. The instrument's role was not hundred percent.

Most importantly, it was simply not possible to carry the whole shebang of laptops, wires, microphones, metal lenses and amplifiers from one place to another.

It was not a gun. Bholaram had thought this to be the only way to eliminate the criminals without any trace. His knees buckled under him in grief.

A simple person and a lovable father. Ankita, realised for the first time that there was a lot of scope in this direction. A sonar gun had not been her idea but now this idea clicked in her mind.

She wanted to seek the help of the monk she had met in Dholavira, but meeting Swami Shivanand was not that easy. And how could he be convinced to help in such a thing?

He was far away, in his Ashram, in a small village near Rajkot. Swami Shivanand passed his time peacefully in a room near Lord Shiva's temple, and he was a busy monk with a monthly schedule of lectures finalized months in advance.

She remembered a business card given by Dr. Mrinal Pandey whom they had met while at the Toran Guest House while visiting Dholavira, the same Professor from IIT, Gandhinagar, who had known Swami Shivanand and had erased their fear about him after a brief introduction.

50.

A heated debate broke out in the house as Santosh had become very angry that the whole affair was being driven through his house. He sensed that Manju and Ankita had developed a soft corner for Nandkishor and Bholaram's families.

The shooting incident at Greater Noida proved to be a trigger and they wanted revenge on behalf of the victims.

'Ankita, you have to focus on your studies and not get involved in such activities. It is a police case and judicial action is needed for justice. We are not party to the whole affair and may get indicted for supporting Bholaram's revenge,' Santosh was vocal in his disapproval.

Manju countered, 'We are not involved. Neither Ankita nor I have any desire for revenge. It is just a coincidence that Bholaram came to our house and that we know him.'

'How can you say that his coming here was a coincidence? He came to keep a watch over you because you met Nandkishor's family, let us be very clear on that. No involvement from now on.'

'Nandkishor saved my life. I am alive today because of him.'

'That's an old story from your childhood, Manju. Don't get so emotional, taking revenge for a crime is not our job and we will be labelled criminals by the law. Our life will become hell.'

'Papa, how can I help them? What Inspector Bholaram Yadav was asking about was my experiment that I had shown him that day. It is useless for any practical purposes.'

'Don't bring your wild ideas and fancies into this. This is the real world, not some virtual world of mythologies. Suppose, Bholaram's plan fails, all the three criminals will recognise us and start chasing us. From hunters, we will become the hunted,' Santosh replied angrily.

It was a clear message that as they smartly presumed to carry on the battle, on the basis of some plan of Bholaram's, they could become the prey.

Santosh left home a little agitated for his daily walk. He had a headache and his eyes were burning.

51.

Manju was agitated beyond words and Ankita was trying to console her. Meeting the two ravaged families had scarred her. The faces of Nandkishor's family and the cries of Bholaram's wife started giving sleepless nights to Manju.

She was unable to come to terms with their loss. Her compassion and pity for the grieving family brought tears to her eyes.

'Ankita, what has happened to me? Santosh is right; we do not have to meddle in these affairs. But can we not help them? What is the harm in helping them?'

'Mom, helping them can land us in big trouble. We will be hounded by criminals and the police for years. We do not know how powerful they are and the people that are helping these criminals. Bholaram, in spite of being a police Sub-Inspector is helpless and he is trying to get us to help him. By now, the entire police force should have been searching for them and arrested the culprits.However, that does not seem to be the case. They have some political clout and are being protected by someone in a high position of power.'

'Ankita, you are perfectly right. I will try to avoid these people and make this drama come out.'

Words seemed to rebel inside Manju. Nandkishor was still on her mind. The memory of her falling into the pond and a young boy running to her rescue flashed in her mind.

Then, there was another little girl, Sakshi coming in her dreams, every day. Worse were the dreams of Sumita crying for her beloved son.

52.

Sumit Bhatnagar silently entered Shloka Society in Sector - 51, Noida. Bhure Lal opened the door. The others were resting on a sofa set. Sumit handed two bags full of groceries to them.

Bhure and his accomplices, Manoj and Mukesh, looked comfortable. Bhure had known Sumit for a number of years. He had saved his life once, and Manoj and Mukesh had met Sumit two years ago and were familiar with him.

Sumit sat on the sofa set. 'What really happened that day, how did you kill Bholaram Yadav's son?'

'We did not intend to kill anybody. You have to check who gave away our whereabouts in Greater Noida.' Bhure was a little angered.

'I have come to know that it was Rohit Srivastava, IG Police of Meerut range, and he somehow got a clue from his intelligence source that is reporting only to him. He has been informed, now he will not create any problem.' Sumit continued, 'Perhaps you don't understand the situation. The murder of a Sub Inspector's son is big news. The entire police department is vigilant.'

'And, him?' Bhure looked straight into his eyes.

'You are alive because of him, Bhure. But there is a limit to it.'

'I know I will get eliminated one day in a police encounter but who cares. I am free till I get caught.' There was no sign of any remorse in Bhure's eyes or voice. Manoj and Mukesh looked at them silently.

Manoj intervened, 'I fired at the Innova on the back side for safety, when a police constable fired on us. I saw a driver, constable and Sub Inspector, we did not expect a young boy to have been sitting there. Whatever has happened has happened, it was the family's destiny.'

Sumit almost fired in anger, 'You will not understand, what happened?'

'So, you want us to understand, ok and if we do not understand, then what?' Bhure also protested. He knew that without Sumit, they may get caught any moment and would have been encountered. Sumit was the safest link between Hem Pratap Singh and them.

Mukesh Kumar looked at them silently and kept staring at them.

Bhure Lal and Sumit Bhatnagar were disturbed this time. It was not just about the crime on Jewar road, they were also worried about the firing in which a policeman's son got killed.

His mobile rang and Sumit responded, 'Yes, I am with them'. The conversation was over.

'Don't worry. That was Surender Nagar, Inspector. He is very close to the Chief Minister.'

'The next time, don't move without informing me and plan in advance. You will be shifted out of Noida after two months. Till then, keep your movements to a minimum.'

'Listen Sumit, we are free. If we get killed in an encounter right now, we don't care.'

'And do you know who those people were who escaped in the car with the third bullet?'

'No, not much concerned.'

'You should, they are friends of Bholaram, a senior government official, and they have registered a FIR with the police.'

Mukesh looked sideways and stared at Manoj for a moment, his eyes did not support the statements made by Bhure.

53.

For Bholaram, the vehicle number of Amaze was the missing link. Not much information could be collected from the name of the owner. It was found to be a fake.

There was no information for a week. In a city with thousands of vehicles, looking for one vehicle that was not plying on the roads frequently was not an easy task.

It was sheer luck, one day, for Bholaram that while driving from the market around nine o'clock in the night to his house, he saw the same car, Honda Amaze, passing by his side and being driven by a younger person. He looked innocent and was talking to someone on the mobile with his earphones plugged in.

Bholaram decided to follow him in his car while maintaining a distance. He almost lost it at the Golf Course Metro Station red light and drove on at a great speed following the last vehicle at the signal. There were no traffic police and for him it was not a matter of concern.

The Amaze slowed down, took a left turn and entered the garage

of Shloka Apartment.
Bholaram decided not to give this information to his superiors.
His mind started formulating a plan.

54.

Bholaram contacted Santosh who did not agree with him. Somehow, he acceded to the request when Bholaram reminded him that he was also a government servant and like him was associated with the security of the nation.

When Santosh met Bholaram for the first time, his sixth sense had liked him for his simplicity. He was a different kind of a policeman. Santosh had a cousin in the police force and even a distant relative in IPS. He was not averse to meeting him, but the idea of a meeting leading to involvement in some crime worried him.

The family sat down for dinner. Bholaram's wife Sumita had come over much to Manju's surprise. The loss of her younger son was written all over her face, the frail figure seemed broken. It was a courtesy meeting and the families shared their experiences.

Santosh and Bholaram sat together and the three women started having corn soup.

Manju told them about Nandkishor saving her life when she had gone to visit her naani. She also talked about meeting the family and helping them financially.

Bholaram was sad and his grief was coming out of his heart. Usually I never picked up my son from Greater Noida after college, it was just sheer coincidence that day.' He was feeling guilty about allowing his son to sit in the police Innova that day. The government had also questioned him about using a police vehicle for personal use.

'I never use the office vehicle for household purposes. I even go to office in my own car, have even taken the bus or metro, but had never taken this facility.'

'Perhaps I have seen one of the men involved in that firing, sitting at the back of the Swift. He was driving an Amaze, and lives near

Sector 51, Shloka Society. They are the same people involved in the Jewar crime incident that had happened in the month of May.'
Santosh was harsh while replying to Bholaram.
'There are hundreds of criminals living in every city now, how the police catch them and take action is up to them. Taking revenge is not anyone's responsibility.'
'I agree with you, but I know my department and I know my superiors.'
'Then what will you do, if you find them?'
'I will kill them.'
'And you will be jailed even if you are a policeman.'
'I know but I want them finished. I will not rest in my life. I have to get justice for my son.'
'My wife Manju also wants to kill them bare handed, for destroy-ing Nandkishor's family. All of them want to be jailed and die a shameful death for the crime of eliminating criminals. They want to become police and judges and be above law. Here, I am sitting with a policeman, who is so helpless and doesn't believe in the system himself.'
'It is not a matter of believing in the system, I know they will escape. I can feel that there are powerful people behind them. It is simply not possible for them to live in Noida, drive a car in the open. It means that someone is helping them from within. If this is the case, they will never be caught. Even if they are caught, they will escape again.'
'How does it concern me?'
'Brother, I know and understand you. The boy who died in the shootout was my son but he could have been anyone.'
'Then, it is so easy for you. You have a gun, the advantage of being in the police and you know their addresses too. You can identify and eliminate them. It is so easy.'
'Yes, I can.'
'Then, who is stopping you.'
'Can it be made a natural death, without gun, without leaving a trace?'
'You tell me, how will you take revenge?'

'With sound.'

Santosh jumped from his chair. 'You are mad. You want my daughter to get involved in this unholy nexus? Listen Bholaram, your son and Nandkishor's family are not my concern at all. I have already explained that my family is not going to fall in any game theory. You close this chapter, and there'll be no further discussion.'

All three women turned to them on hearing Santosh shouting. He was literally mad.

Bholaram decided not to protest or say anything. He knew that he had put the idea forward and the results would be slow to come.

Ankita was looking at him bewildered. Her simple act of showing a fun experiment of moving thermocol balls with sound to Bholaram some time ago was leading him to take revenge with that method.

Perhaps he was not aware of her real pursuit of infrasonic gun.

That gun if ever made could be useful.

Ankita decided to make one with whatever little knowledge she had acquired. Dr. Jatin might help at least in guiding in the initial stages.

The topic of their conversation became more general. Sumita was looking sad and broken. Manju and Ankita were silent, and Santosh called them for dinner.

It was a quick dinner and both the families exchanged greetings and the guests departed.

Santosh just slumped on his sofa set. Destiny, he thought for a second, was beyond his control.

He had become party to events that were not related to him or his family and he was worried.

55.

Sumit Bhatnagar and Surender Nagar sat in Greater Noida, the area was not crowded and was favoured by both of them.

It was a sparsely populated society parallel to the expressway.

Sumit always liked the isolation of jungles and remote places. He was not a man who liked crowds, it was his nature, and he followed a yearly routine of living in far off jungles in India, disappearing from his stressful work for a fortnight.

'So, what is the plan for this year?' Surender was curious. The last place suggested by him was liked a lot by his wife, Krishna. Shivamogga in Karnataka with its jungles and Jog Falls was enjoyed to the hilt by the Nagar family.

'Koraput in Odisha. I will go after this matter gets resolved.' Sumit replied.

'This time, the situation is a little tense after Bholaram's son got killed accidentally. It was difficult to convince even Hem Pratap Singh that this was a coincidence.'

'He and the party chief do not want to lose them till elections next year. After that, no one is concerned about what happens to them.'

'Bhure Lal knows this part of the story. He knows all too well that he is being protected till elections, all the facilities and protection are telling him the truth. However, his accomplices are not that seasoned. I do not know from where he picked them up. I have only known them for two years.'

'Why did they do whatever they did at Jewar? Bhure is mad; he should not have gotten involved in this. His real value is in carrying out his boss's orders, not petty crimes. He is a professional, how can he do this?'

Sumit was sceptical and cautioned him. 'Bholaram is very silent these days, what is going on in his mind?'

'Nothing, he is sad. He seems to have accepted his fate.'

'Poor fellow, using the police vehicle for personal use cost him his son's life.'

'Any news about the Nandkishor family?'

'They are very poor. Nandkishor was the main source of income for the family. Now his son is trying to set up his business but the family is destroyed. Usually, they do not come out of their house in Mamura.'

'Anything in particular.'

'Yes, a lady came to visit them twice but nothing in particular. Perhaps she is connected with Nandkishor's village somehow. Not much is known and there has been no contact after that.'
Sumit ignored the idea. She could be a well-wisher of the family, some old contact or a compassionate visitor.
Sumit took out two glasses and a 100 Pipers bottle. It was his go-to brand, whenever he was entertaining Surender or anyone else. He was not an alcoholic but enjoyed the company, and he knew it helped in generating business and contacts.

56.

Next morning sitting in her flat's balcony, Ankita's thoughts vibrated with the words 'sound' and 'Bholaram'. Sometimes messages may come from 'unexpected' corners.
Even if there was a remote possibility of helping him, how would she travel with all the bulky equipment and focussing objects? It was a weird idea.
She always wanted to make it portable and easy to carry - the oscillations multiplier and see the effects on objects or even animals.
She needed some help, as she was lost in her thoughts when she picked up the newspaper.
She turned the pages of the newspaper. In the Noida section, there was a small advertisement for celebrations and lectures on Raas Leela by Swami Shivanand of Shiva Ashram Gondal.
Swamiji in Noida, the same monk she had met in Dholavira. She ran to tell her mom.
Her mom was ready to attend the function. It was in the evening from 7:00 to 8:00 pm and both of them decided not to miss the opportunity.

57.

When Manju told him about the presence of Swami Shivanand in

Noida, Santosh was also overwhelmed. He suggested inviting him home for refreshments, provided he agreed and had a comfortable time schedule.

The programme started at 7:00 pm the next day in one of the nearby temples. There was an audience of about two hundred people waiting for him.

Swami Shivanand sat on the dais, with two disciples and a mike. The temperature and ambience of the hall was cosy and very soothing to the eyes.

Swamiji delivered a lecture on Lord Krishna's Raas Leela, his words slowly started graduating from the dance of Gopis to the dance of nature and then dance of electrons around the nucleus of an atom.

People were mesmerized. Very few had ever heard about the relation of Heisenberg's Uncertainty Principle with Raas Leela of Lord Krishna and the divine dance on the night of Sharad Purnima.

Manju expressed her desire of meeting him in person and extending an invitation to dinner at home. One of the helps present in the temple was doubtful whether he would accept the offer. He however allowed both of them to meet him.

After the lecture, Manju and Ankita waited silently for their turn to meet him. Swami Shivanand recognised them and flashed the same enigmatic smile.

'Swamiji, we met in Dholavira.'

'Yes Ankita, I remember. You were with your father. How is he?'

'Swamiji, we would like to invite you for dinner at our home.' Manju was prompt, she knew that it somebody else came, it would break the conversation.

'Swamiji, I want to talk to you for some time. Please don't say no,' Ankita was literally begging him to accept the invitation.

Two of the disciples were amused, and started looking like they expected the answer to be no. Swamiji rarely went to the houses of disciples. 'Swamiji, I have some doubts about sound and its effects on bodies, I will show you my work and collection of ancient literature on sound. I will show you my research and even an experiment to show the real effect of convergence of sound from Dholavira and Prabhas Kshetra, Veraval and change of mediums. It works, please come home.' Ankita was requesting him humbly.

Swami Shivanand was himself a doctorate in physics. He had delivered a number of lectures on physics and spiritualism; he was very much a believer in the powers of mantra in healing bodies and mind.

He thought for a moment, and asked one of his disciples, 'What is the programme for tomorrow?'

'We have a get together with the locals followed by one more lecture and we may be free by seven in the evening.'

'Manju, no dinner for me. However, I will come to your house with one of the disciples to have a word with your intelligent and extraordinary daughter. May God bless her! Why will I break my child's heart? You see, we have a flight back to Ahmedabad the day after tomorrow morning at eight o'clock, and I need to make some preparations. Please allow us to leave by 9:30 pm positively. I will take some fruits, nothing more,' then Swamiji turned to the next visitor.

Manju and Ankita wished him, and gave their house address to his disciple with contact details. He was watching them with a lot of curiosity.

58.

Swami Shivanand was a little early, almost by fifteen minutes. Somehow, he got some time and decided to spend it with Santosh's family. Santosh welcomed the Swamiji and his disciple. 'Namaskar Swamiji. It is a great honour for us to invite you to our house. I hope your stay in Noida was comfortable. We remember meeting you in Dholavira and spoke about you all the time while travelling in Gujarat. Ankita remembers you a lot.' Santosh was very happy now.

'We will come to your ashram in Junagadh and stay there for some time.' Manju added and supported the words of her husband.

Swami Shivanand sat comfortably on the sofa. He was smiling. He had found a humble family with a scientific temperament. He always liked people with reason and logic, families who support their children in the endeavour of learning. His lectures to promote the discipline and capacity to learn beyond boundaries were famous in schools. Even a number of corporate had called him for stress management lectures, adding value to business decisions and surviving failure.

Ankita was looking at him with curiosity, ready to start the conversation and waiting for her turn. Santosh saw his daughter's face and smiled. Manju left them to cut and arrange for fruits and juice.

'So finally; I am here, Ankita. I will listen to you first and then we will have a discussion', the Swamiji smiled at her.

'I will show you my collection of books and equipment, research and results.' Ankita said almost jumping with joy.

Finally, all the four entered the room specially dedicated to her endeavours.

It was a medium-sized room in the flat with five almirahs, all full of books, a long table, computers, a mesh of wires, soldering machines, almost fifty speakers of different sizes, microprocessors, microphones, a number of tiny unknown small machines, lenses made of different metals, pendulums, oscillators, forks of different sizes, transducers, dilators and many more. The room looked as chaotic as a small-sized factory or a repair workshop.

The Swamiji was baffled. He had not imagined such a level of investment in books and in setting up a lab by a father for his daughter.

The Swamiji was silent, as he started observing the books in the almirah, covering Vedas, Upanishads, research papers, ancient literatures, one almirah full of spiral-bound pages that must have been independent research papers downloaded from the internet. For the first time in his life, he had seen such a level of rigour beyond college facilities.

'What really triggered you to explore in this direction? It is very unusual. I have met so many young students but found none who pursues physics in mythology with such rigour.'

'I am fascinated with stories of wars between Devas and Asuras, kings and demons, and the use of sound as a war medium between them. They used to chant mantras and fight with ordinary equipment. How did the simple mantras transform ordinary weapons into mean machines?'

'Where have you reached now and what are your questions?' the Swamiji was a little concerned and amused.

'Is it possible to move objects with sound?'

'I think you have already experimented with it.'

'It is so difficult, with so much equipment. I want to make a simple hand-held instrument that is easy to carry,' Ankita replied.

The Swamiji thought for a second, 'If I understand correctly, they used the concept of understanding natural vibrations of objects, enemies, animals or weapons and then received them with the mind or some other invention that we don't understand today. After analysing the frequencies, they chanted and recited the mantra, giving that enormous power to their weapons. It was receiving the natural frequency of people and objects first, and then modifying them. Look at the source of the origin of sound. It is the reason for our existence, our life as well as our destruction.'

Ankita looked a little confused; it was an angle she had not thought of. She had always concentrated on projecting the manufactured sound waves from the laptop on objects through a series of processors.

The Swamiji continued, 'Ankita, you have to think in a new direction. You will find an answer to your questions. We live in a fast-changing world, but if we stick to basic tenets of life, we can always find a solution. Keep moving my daughter. You have come a long way and have a life to live and love.'

The Swamiji and his disciple left the room with Santosh and Ankita.

They were once again in the drawing room, and time was running out fast. Ankita decided not to disturb him with any more questions. She was more than happy about the short and unexpected visit. It was more than she had asked for.

Manju served fruit delicacies and fresh mausambi juice to every-one.

The conversation changed to general topics and Santosh started discussing his personal job profile and meditation techniques.

Swamiji suggested some tips to practice silence for the mind in the busy life of NCR. Ankita was silent and listened carefully. The Swamiji thanked them and said goodbye.

Santosh and Ankita decided to take a walk in the society's park discussing college and other matters.

Manju jumped to watch TV; it was time for her favourite serial.

59.

Bholaram was shocked when he saw the three of them in the market with the same Amaze, near a police vehicle. The patrolling jeep drove away slowly.

Bholaram decided to stay there. He was not in his uniform and was not in an official car. He decided to watch from a distance and recognised the person driving the Swift that day.

He felt the urge to immediately tell the control office, but he knew it would be late, and he had a plan in his mind.

He needed to act fast and take help. He wanted to take revenge and wanted to eliminate them without a trace.

In addition, he did not want to involve anybody except An-kita. Why Ankita, he again asked himself, he could not answer.

Bholaram was a good shooter and had an official revolver with him, ready for any action.

Two things were confirmed, all the three were in Noida, second he knew the society but who else knew.

He decided to find out. It was very important for him, who in the echelons of power was helping them to stay so fearlessly in Noida. There was a mole in the local police and someone else also who was well known.

The next morning, he decided to go jogging on the street in a track suit in front of Shloka Society.He was sweating like a runner, he slowed down, and it was around seven o'clock in the morning.

He saw someone coming out of the society gate wearing trousers and a shirt with a black coat on, generally worn by lawyers accompanied by Mukesh Kumar. They were talking slowly and then, Mukesh left immediately.

Sumit Bhatnagar was scanning the road. He had found nothing unusual, except that one middle-aged person had taken a U-turn near the society and was coming back.

Bholaram crossed him, without giving a glimpse, jogging in a normal style, but Sumit noticed him, saw his face clearly and registered it in his mind.

Sumit started his car, an old Honda City and drove away. He was late for work and wanted to meet Surender Nagar in the office on some other case.

He reached there around 11 am. Inspector Surender Nagar was busy with some local visitors who had a complaint, and Sumit sat down near him, looking at him.

It was at that time that Bholaram wanted to discuss some work with Surender Nagar. Sumit was staring at Surender who was talking to visitors, Bholaram entered the room and no one noticed for a moment.

There he saw Sumit, the same person he had seen today while jogging with the third criminal.

He turned around and returned to the door. Surender was still busy, he noticed but ignored. He decided to skip meeting him as Sumit was there.

Bholaram was raging inside, his immediate superior was somehow linked with the criminals and perhaps protecting them.

Now it was more complicated than he had imagined at first.

He knew very well that Surender was a close associate of Hem Pratap Singh due to his father's affiliations, DGP and many more in the political circles. He knew the background of his father and that he was involved in a number of matters that no one knew of.

He controlled himself as the face of his young son cameto his mind, lying in a pool of blood in the patrolling car that day. Three people in the Swift and all three were present in Noida. Perhaps his superior, Surender Nagar was involved in the matter, perhaps he knew it all.

What to do now? His mind and heart were racing. He took a glass of water, came out of the office and started moving around. Some colleagues joined him for discussions.

He tried to avoid the anger in his heart and started talking. Now he was sure about his sixth sense and wanted to implement the plan in his mind. The faster the better.

60.

Bholaram was lying awake in his room. It was 2 a.m. and sleep was a thousand miles away from his eyes and suddenly his elder son opened the door.

After a long time, there were tears in his eyes. He started crying remembering his younger son.

His elder son, Shobhit was studying computer science from the National Institute of Technology, Jaipur and was to leave the next day for his college after his holidays that he had taken due to household problems.

Bholaram narrated all the incidents, meeting all the three cul-prits, about Sumit, Surender, and Ankita and her research.

Shobhit could not make out anything the first time. How was Ankita connected to all this in his father's mind, but he got some clue of a technical innovation that his father was talking about.

Shobhit decided to stay for one more day and meet Ankita in person.

61.

Sumit Bhatnagar was involved in some more cases with Surender Nagar, but was not seen with him too often.

Bholaram decided to keep a watch on his movements, and finally engaged one of his young constables for the job. Now Sumit's movements, his known persons were on his radar.

In the meantime, Shobhit met Ankita. Hesitant to start with, however she opened her room to him and tried to explain the concepts of her research.

Her idea of catching natural vibrations of objects, living beings and amplifying them appealed to Shobhit, his mind started racing about the reference by his father and why he was interested in the research. His father was not a science person, but how was he thinking of using it, remained a mystery.

He further tried to understand what exactly Ankita was attempting.

Ankita explained in the words of Swami Shivanand about natural vibrations, mythological concepts and use of mantras in wars.

Shobhit took her as a fanciful girl, who was just pursuing a hobby to pass time.

'You know Ankita, every object, building, living being and equipment are vibrating with natural frequency, and it is a well-known truth. However, catching their natural vibrations, and amplifying them with power and returning them can create a destructive effect if the objects are not strong enough. Plenty of material is available on the internet, you can watch YouTube videos for long hours but you will still not reach a conclusion.'

'Are you talking about a sonic gun?'

'It works on loud sound, whereas you are working on low, almost inaudible sounds, natural vibrations.'

'Everything's wrong with me,' Ankita just fumed.

'No, I am just trying to help you,' Shobhit tried to control the situation sensing a little uneasiness.

'Catching the natural vibrations and striking them back with amplified amplitude and pitch within seconds.'

'To capture an isolated sound in thousands of objects, and processing it will take a number of machines, you can't use it till you have a handheld device.'

Ankita was puzzled for a moment, the boy was some years younger to her, but showed an unusual way of thinking.

'What are you pursuing, hardware or software in computers?'

'Both, Ankita. I can help you, if you tell me your ideas.'

'Ok, I will show you a concept in the making.'
Ankita brought one small barrel made of copper. The barrel was almost eight inches long and around one and a half inches in diameter.
'I want to fit in the whole concept in this barrel.' Ankita then showed the basic idea of fitting batteries to power mini microphones, a circuit board that Shobhit could not understand but could make out as a processor for modifying the captured sounds, one small mother board and three to four metal lenses, one peculiar small dish type radar with many hair-line thin wires attached with a port at the bottom of the tiny stand it was holding. The whole concept revolved around hearing the vibrations and then reverting.
Shobhit was mesmerized, it was leading to quite an unusual experiment at the mini-home lab. Terrific work, he thought for a moment, his electronics-engineering friends would go mad after seeing these efforts, that too without any support. It must be the year's effort to design and build this small equipment.
'I think your father wants a gun without any trace, any fire, and a technique that will not be available in the market even in the remote future.'
Shobhit was taken aback. The girl understood why he was here. Ankita was staring at him with cold eyes. His face had a cold expression.
'I can make it but I may need a little help from you.'
Shobhit literally jumped to his feet. 'I am ready.'
'When are you going back?'
'Tomorrow morning by Pink City Express.'
'Then go, you will take a lot of time to understand the basic concepts, just keep it to yourself. We will discuss after some time, when you get a little more conversant with the effects of sounds, and do some meditation.'
Shobhit returned home and told Bholaram that what he had planned had a rare chance of succeeding but if made, he would like to help him in his mission.
Santosh was not worried and ignored the information. Manju

liked the boy and did not mind him meeting Ankita. He was almost three to four years younger than her daughter and seemed to be cultured and was Bholaram's son. She had some pity and empathy.

62.

Bhure, Manoj and Mukesh were trying to pass time by keeping a low profile, their attire was changed, clothes and hairstyle was a lot more different from earlier. However, in spite of Sumit's warning, walking on the streets of Noida and shopping was their favourite pastime.

Bhure had already mentioned his intention to leave the group for the time being. He thought it was dangerous for all three of them to be in one place and now there was no need of it.

His wife had also called him several times and his young son was creating a ruckus in the house about his absence. Bhure decided to visit his house next week after arranging money.

Sumit used to supply the requirements as and when required. It was all assignment based. However, the accidental death of Bholaram's son had created a lot of problems even for Sumit to convince his superiors in Lucknow.

Bhure Lal left with the promise to return after fifteen days.

63.

Ankita cut the copper barrel in five parts and soldered four flanges in them for re-joining these parts with screws.

The process started as she fitted miniature parts in the barrel, one after another with ninety parts assembled in the five pieces of copper barrels, with space for the batteries.

It was her second day. Fitting it with minute details and hand-soldering was very tedious. Santosh tried to make some conversation while she explained the details. Manju was a little amused but not much concerned and as usual she was engrossed in TV and her favourite serials. Santosh was leaving for two days to Jaisalmer on some official work.

She needed plenty of time without any disturbances. It was Ankita's free time. After returning from college, she closeted herself in her room.

The first attempt started in the night around eleven. She kept a tuning fork standing on a small tripod on the table at a two-metre distance from the tightly held barrel on another tripod. She connected the USB port from the copper barrel with her laptop and another self-built port on the other end with the wires coming out from a microphone at the base of the tuning fork to record changing frequencies.

The experiment started; she stroked the tuning fork with a wooden mallet lightly. The barrel perfectly in alignment with the fork was recording all the signals properly.

After four to five minutes, the tuning fork stopped looking like it was vibrating, but she knew it was still in motion as a different range was appearing on her laptop screen.

She took a deep breath, and clicked the remote, the resonance matched in the fraction of a second and the barrel bombarded back the same frequency with manifold power.

Nothing happened. The sensor at the base of the tuning fork did not record any changes.

It was the end of the day, time to sleep.

64.

Sumit came to meet Manoj and Mukesh on a regular basis. He knew that Bhure might return in a fortnight or may not return at all. He wanted to change the location.

Bholaram deployed one more constable to keep a watch over him and by chance the security-in-charge of Shloka Society was from the same village as the constable. With due respect to the policeman, he decided to keep a watch, record timings, make a list of people meeting them and inform any change in status. The third person had left, he informed the constable.

There was nothing abnormal to notice, both looked at ease and they informed the security guard that they were looking for a job in Noida.

65.

Somehow, out of the blue an idea clicked in Ankita's mind and she made a video of her experiment with the copper barrel again, wrote a note, photographed the internal parts and diagrams and forwarded it to Shobhit by e-mail.

Shobhit could not make much of it as sound was not his domain and he was learning computer science. He decided to involve his close electronics-engineering friend studying in the college.

Shobhit decided to explore and kept on thinking about who uses natural vibrations most by means of reverberations coming back from the hurdles and objects.

It came to him like a flash. Bats, yes bats use the frequencies and sound mechanism that is not audible to human ears as they navigate in the dark.

'Is your barrel capable of capturing the frequencies of bats and can you pass messages with bats?' After two days, he wrote to Ankita.

She had never thought of it. Ankita was perplexed, any idea was welcome, how much ever absurd it may seem at first.

But how does one catch a bat, there were none in the society. There was a temple in the nearby village where bats would hang from a peepal tree. Not many but there were some.

Before leaving with the barrel, fork and laptop, she decided to check the power of batteries, it was empty. She replaced it and decided to add a power indicator with battery symbol on it.

She checked it again holding the barrel and tuning fork. It was so easy; within seconds the battery went from hundred percent to zero.

Ankita stopped the exercise and left for dinner. Helping her mother in the kitchen for some time was a better proposition to relieve stress. She never missed it.

Manju smiled at her. 'So finally, some time for mother also. You know Nandkishor's family has conveyed their thanks for our help during their difficult time.'

'It is good, mom. You are always kind to everyone.'

'I still remember Nandkishor in my dreams. The boy running to help me while I was drowning in the pond, I could never have been here with all of you today had he not saved my life.' Manju was sad again.

'Mom, there are hundreds of people we meet in life, some are good, some are bad. It is a simple unforgiving fact of life,' Ankita tried to console her.

'There is no news about the whereabouts of the criminals who killed Nandkishor and you know the police are so clueless. When a person like Bholaram is helpless, how can an ordinary citizen get justice?' Manju was in the mood to talk on the subject while preparing dinner. It was around eight in the evening and Santosh was on his way.

'Yes mom, and there is no way we can help them.'

'How is his son, who had come to meet you? What was he saying?"

'He wanted to understand the nature of my experiments.'

'How does it interest him? Is he studying physics?'

'No, he is studying computer science from NIT in Jaipur, but he is intelligent and understands things fast.'

'Yes, his younger brother is lost to them without a reason, because of a little foolishness. I don't know why government servants use office vehicles for personal use.' Manju raised her voice a little.

Santosh as was his routine reached home at eight thirty in the night and got ready for dinner. It was his habit to take dinner as fast as possible and then go on a leisurely walk with his family in the society park. Everyone knew it and he used to meet the residents only there with his busy schedule.

Ankita checked her mobile, a new mail flashed from Shobhit. She read it. 'I think the batteries will get discharged very fast.

The capacitors in the circuit board are connected incorrectly and perhaps the barrel is also drawing current. Fix it before any further experiments.' Then he suggested with some drawing on the circuit board, highlighting the same pattern as was discussed with one of his electronics engineering friends.

Tomorrow, Ankita thought for a second and joined her father for a walk in the society park.

66.

Ankita's main worry was about how she could make sound waves behave like a beam of light. It was a well-known fact that sound tends to be omni-directional or spreading out like a fan.

Capturing a natural vibration from thousands of frequencies and then amplifying it with manifold power for the fraction of a second before hitting a target was really a challenge.

The bats, Ankita was now thinking of the idea, and then as Shobhit said, she needed to fix the power discharge problem by some capacitor arrangement. One of the transducers may also need some change. The transducer was modified for all ranges, from low infrasonic to ultrasonic frequencies.

She was in a fix. However, she opened the barrel again and changed the capacitors' arrangement as suggested by Shobhit and changed the connections and insulated them with the barrel body more effectively.

She attempted once more with the tuning fork with variable frequencies, the batteries survived with several attempts, but the forks did not reverberate with a reply from the barrel.

Something was not conceptually correct, Ankita thought. After all, the world over, research in huge universities' facilities, military labs and research organisations, all have failed. There was nothing for her to worry about.

After changes and attending to the charge leakage problems, she went to the local temple. There were hardly any bats there. Then she found one, flying fast, and vanishing into thin air within seconds.

There was the sound of bells, and she flashed her torch at the branches of the peepal tree. It looked fearful.

Silently, she took out the barrel, fastened a tripod and flashed the torchlight on a bat hanging from the tree.

The bat didn't like the light. It came fast towards Ankita. She almost wanted to run away, but somehow started the charge and clicked the button. The ultrasonic frequency was captured by the barrel, there was also a sound of the temple bell and then the barrel was silent in less than five seconds. There was a minor audible beep and the bat was nowhere to be seen. She found it lying down near the barrel, a meter away.

The small creature was lying at a distance from Ankita. She threw some light on it but the bat did not move.

Ankita packed up and almost went running from the site.

She mailed the outcome to Shobhit and wrote about the bat incident. Shobhit planned to visit Noida the next Saturday.

He kept wondering whether the experiment would work at low range frequencies. If he was able to change it somehow, he could accomplish his mission.

67.

Manju, was taken aback by the presence of Shobhit at her door. She knew that Ankita and he were doing some experiments but to welcome him again did not appeal to her at that time.

'Who is at the door, mom?'

'It is Shobhit. I think he has come to meet you.'

Her mother's voice and tone made Ankita a little uncomfortable. After taking a cup of tea, they moved to the mini lab and started talking.

Manju informed Santosh about Shobhit's presence at their house and that they were talking about some experiment. Santosh comforted her, the boy was probably just fascinated with science like Ankita and there was nothing to worry about.

Ankita unfolded the barrel and took out all the parts one by one. After talking for a long time and changing the concept of ultrasonic to infrasonic boom and reverberations, Shobhit suggested they add one more microprocessor and frequencies' modulator. However, the question was about where to fit them. Finally, Ankita took the decision to add another two inches long part to the barrel.

They again fitted the barrel on the tripod and tuning fork and the simple experiment was repeated again in the presence of Shobhit. The tuning fork was almost silent, the laptops were recording the infra range of vibrations and weak signals.

'Now, press the button', Shobhit who was sitting by one of the laptops, clicked the mouse on the bells being repeated on the screen. Ankit pressed a small button on the remote. The fork seemed to hum and the microphone recording the sound at the base of the fork sent the signals to another laptop.

The barrel was again receiving the signals. Ankita pressed the button once more.

The sound this time was clear and audible. Ankita kept changing the pace and timings and again the results were the same. Her biggest riddle and years of efforts was successful, of course with Shobhit's help.

She was happy, very happy and was talking in a rush. Manju entered the room hearing loud voices and saw the happy face of her daughter.

'Mom, I have made it.' Ankita was full of joy.

Manju looked at the boy. He was sitting silently, looking at both of them without any expression and his eyes seemed lost.

After lunch, Shobhit left the flat with words of congratulations and warm wishes, with the simple idea of capturing the natural vibrations and seeing the results.

Ankita wasn't in the mood to listen to anything now.

68.

Shobhit could not sleep that night. Was it a sound gun that he had read about so many times on the internet? There was so much more hidden in the wires of the barrel and laptop that only Ankita knew about. When she pressed the remote, she seemed to have made a humming sound, almost like chanting a mantra.

When he pressed the remote button several times in excitement, nothing happened. There was something more to this experiment, perhaps he would never know.

Even if there was a remote possibility, would she like to be a part of the plan that his father Bholaram was concocting? Would it not tantamount to being involved in murder and if ever caught then it would lead to punishment by the law?

Bholaram was shocked after hearing about the news of the barrel, about the bat incident and now about the low frequency reverberations. He always thought about it, the time he had seen it in Ankita's house, while she had shown him the jumping of that thermocol ball by a speaker's sound.

With every passing day, his heart was filling with vengeance. After he saw Sumit Bhatnagar in Surender Nagar's office, and Sumit with those three criminals in Shloka Society, so close to his house, the thought of them being protected by his own police department, the involvement of his seniors and political bosses made him want to shoot all of them without any remorse. The Jewar incident was sufficient for their death penalty and now his beloved son was dead. He wanted to be a judge and executor all rolled into one.

How could he convince Ankita and her family to help him? The last time too, Santosh had understood his intentions and vehemently protested and prevented them from moving in that direction.

He would not have allowed his own daughter to fall into this trap but his heart was on fire and his elder son's involvement in the story was growing in his mind.

Shobhit was clear, young and energetic and he wanted to help his father.

Both father and son decided to discuss the matter at length, planning and executing the plot.

Finally, it revolved around getting the confidence of Ankita, doing some more experiments and seeing the results and whether it really works as Shobhit wanted or was it all just a waste of time.

69.

Manju was furious with the two rats running around her flat. She was surprised about how they had reached to such a height.

'What do you do all day, just killing time when you can't even kill a rat?' Manju started laughing at Ankita.

'I am not a rat killer.'

'Ok, we shall go to the market in the evening and bring a rat trap or Rat-Kill. These two rats have been creating a lot of nuisance all day.'

However, Ankita had another problem. One of the rats was running around in her little lab and chewing the wires, which was a problem for her too.

She took out the barrel, and started looking for them in the house. There was no trace of them, but she heard a sound in the kitchen.

Ankita closed the kitchen door and started removing the utensils. In a corner, she found one hiding and ready to run.

She held the machine in her hand, and switched on the power, trying to capture the natural frequencies. The rat was now looking in her direction. With the kitchen door closed and the ground clean, it was ready to jump anywhere.

After fifteen seconds, Ankita pressed the remote button she was holding in another hand, pointing the barrel towards the rat.

The rat ran towards her, she panicked for a moment and opened the kitchen door, shouting for her mom. The rat ran towards the drawing room, and then suddenly stopped moving.

Manju and Ankita looked bewildered.

'What happened?'

Ankita pointed towards the brass barrel in her hand. The rat had died on the floor. Ankita was surprised. Perhaps, she had made a sound gun with infra or low-level frequencies.

Santosh laughed like hell in the evening. Who knew whether the rat died of fear or hunger?

70.

Shobhit decided to understand the basics of resonance. He started reading the literature collected.

First, it was clear to him that sound is an energy and could be used to make a weapon, a directional device. The infrasonic generator could shoot a person and create fear, anxiety, and even damage the organs. The range of 3 Hz to 20 Hz could be the reason. How to hear it?

The power or decibel of the organs in the body of any living animal cannot be heard from a distance. However, it remains a fact that all the chemical reactions in the cells of living organisms are caused by electromagnetic oscillations, pulsations and vibrations. All physical matter is vibrating at its own frequency. Once resonance is achieved with that natural frequency, it will affect the tissue permanently.

Sound can be used to shatter or explode objects after resonance has been achieved.

Therefore, the trick lies in first listening to the natural frequency of the organs inside the body and then capturing it with radar.

Infrasound travels great distances and can easily pass through most buildings and vehicles. 100 to 140 dB infrasound causes a variety of biological symptoms including vibrations of internal organs to severe intestinal pain. Higher power levels can liquefy the bowels and cause death.

He wanted to check one part of the barrel made by Ankita and see the result. Can it also have a small radar, first sending a signal, catching the natural frequency and then giving the information back to the system that further generates the impulse within the fraction of a second?

If it worked, then his job would be over.

Ankita ignored his questions. Shobhit was not supposed to know everything. It was dangerous and she knew the implications.

71.

Ankita informed her father about the results.
Santosh was silent for five minutes, looking at her and trying to understand the whole scenario.
'Suppose, we agree to help him and it doesn't work at that moment, what will happen?'
'Nobody can catch me for carrying a barrel that no one understands. There will be no proof about whatever happens to any one, if it works.'
'If your action fails, and if they realise who we are and plan a counter attack, the police will not be able to help us. Bholaram knows where they are hiding, and even his own superior is helping them. What are the chances that we will not become a part of this intrigue?'
'If we succeed, will there be a backlash?'
'No, I don't think so. They may allow us to escape and live peacefully forever, as they will find many others to do their jobs. The gang is a burden for them, they may get eliminated after some time by the same police team that is protecting them.'
'I will not fail, but I will not go ahead without your consent.'
'Ankita, you are our only child and my only hope for living this life. Manju had a very difficult time during child birth.' Santosh was looking contemplatively.
'Papa, what is the worst that can happen. I could have lost you during the Greater Noida shootout, when Bholaram's son died. Given a choice, I would like to help Bholaram and bring justice to Nandkishor's family. If I fail, then I will leave these fanciful experiments and devote my time to other fields. I'll take on life straight and get married or even leave for a prestigious institute to do my PhD. I have left many opportunities in the past.'
Santosh realised that Ankita had indeed ignored all the charms of

IITs and even left Delhi University for the sake of making time for her mother.

Santosh replied, 'Give me time till morning to think and I will confirm.'

Santosh kept on deliberating with Manju almost the whole night, weighing the pros and cons.

In the middle of the night, he called Bholaram at his home and they again deliberated the matter. The entire Bholaram family were also at the risk of being wiped away. They could not afford failure.

Santosh woke up late in the morning and Ankita had already left for college. She had known the answer that night itself that it was time for action now.

72.

Santosh strictly told Bholaram to keep distance. In his company, the chances of Ankita getting hurt in any way were very high.

Finally, Ankita, Shobhit and his father Bholaram made a play for it, it was decided that she'd be given almost ten minutes for action and within half an hour, she would be dropped back home.

73.

Bholaram was sure that around eight o'clock in the morning, one of them would come out for a drive every day.

Moreover, he was right. The Amaze was on the road with Manoj Kumar driving the vehicle.

Now the task was to pass the vehicle on the right side with Ankita sitting on the left and running parallel to the Amaze for thirty seconds steadily.

It was a slow drive, no need to hurry. As Ankita passed the Amaze, she raised the barrel in the direction of the driver and kept looking straight and focussed. It was five seconds of reverting back to low frequency vibrations that confirmed the heartbeat of the

Amaze driver on the laptop.

She just pressed the button with a deep voice and long humming in a microphone attached near her neck. When the car passed the Amaze, it was still driving.

'Move and don't look back,' Ankita cried.

Bholaram was not sure; he wanted to see what had happened.

'Move', Ankita cried, 'He is gone.'

There was a sudden pain in Manoj Kumar's chest and it was increasing. Within a minute he collapsed at the wheel itself. The Amaze stopped slowly.

People were looking at the wavering car and started getting restless with the traffic holdup.

Police reached the site within twenty minutes and a dead body was taken out of the car.

There was no clue about the cause of death. After three days' autopsy, the post-mortem report decided it was a sudden heart attack. Mukesh Kumar was shocked and he almost fainted. They had taken some liquor the last night and Manoj had been a little disturbed and had taken more than his capacity, he had not been well at night too.

Perhaps, it was an overdose and the liquor had reacted.

Sumit Bhatnagar didn't think it was normal. Manoj had died for unknown and very different reasons, and it was not a normal and natural death. A heart attack at his age for a healthy person like Manoj Kumar?

74.

Surender Nagar sensed something was unusual and was crying hoarsely. He made repeated calls to someone in Lucknow. His wife, Krishna, had never seen him so out of control since marriage. He had been made in charge of the security of all the three by Hem Pratap Singh himself, how was this possible?

It was an unusual case, where some insiders were trying to protect and in that case, an encounter by police and rivals was out of question. There may be some factors that may not be clear in the first instance.

Surender immediately discussed with Sumit that Mukesh should be shifted out of the society flat, even sent back to his hometown. Sumit Bhatnagar discussed it with Mukesh. He was hesitant and needed strong support to stay in Noida. With Manoj not on the scene due to his sudden demise and Bhure Lal not likely to return, he agreed to return to his hometown. Once he left Noida, the situation might change dramatically.

He thought over repeatedly but could not reach a conclusion about how Manoj died of a heart attack while driving a car. He was a robust and healthy man. Did someone poison him but he had been with him all the time since they had come to Noida.

Outside food at doubtful locations was out of question. They had never met anyone except Sumit, and some security guards of the society, that too they had avoided to the extent possible.

The next day Mukesh decided to leave. Sumit discussed with him and they agreed that he would be leaving by a roadways bus to his hometown near Agra.

The security guard of Shloka Society intimated Bholaram about this development. Perhaps one of the residents was planning to leave the city the next day morning by bus.

75.

Sumit stopped his vehicle at the main bus stand entrance. He found Bholaram and a girl with a flute-like object, a bag and a newspaper.

She seemed to be his relative, being dropped at the bus stand. Nevertheless, the presence of Bholaram created a sense of unease in his mind.

Sumit was extra cautious and was worried after the sudden demise of Manoj. Was it natural or had something happened to him? The post-mortem report did not reveal any symptoms, the heart just collapsed, with some veins ruptured.

Sumit and Mukesh entered Sector 37 Noida bus stand.

Bholaram looked away, Ankita was trying to read the newspaper, holding the barrel in her hand with all its decorative beads and coloured threads.

The bus was ready and the driver brought his bus near the exit, ready to go.

Sumit confirmed the seat in the bus and came down. The seat was next to the conductor's on the window side.

They were talking to each other. The driver started honking. It would have taken hardly thirty seconds to board the bus.

The driver honked again. Sumit and Mukesh held each other's hands for some time.

Mukesh turned and moved towards the bus.

Ankita was exactly opposite him, Sumit was watching Mukesh. Mukesh tried to ignore her but somehow, she caught his attention and smiled and he smiled back. Sumit looked back in her direction.

Ankita pressed the button raising the barrel towards Mukesh's chest.

Mukesh jumped into the bus as it started.

Perhaps it was late, perhaps it was not. Bholaram just whispered to Ankita, 'Move'.

Sumit was looking at the bus moving slowly, he saw the pain-stricken face of Mukesh.

He looked back, no one was there, and he jumped into the slowly moving bus.

He cried, 'Mukesh.'

There was no reply. The bus conductor and other passengers started looking at him. The bus was near a U-turn.

'Mukesh', Sumit shouted as loudly as possible and found Mukesh slumped in his seat.

The bus driver stopped the bus after the U-turn towards the side.

There was a hue and cry by fellow passengers since a passenger had just died while in his seat.

Sweat started rolling down Sumit's face as he informed Surender Nagar.

76.

Surender was getting ready when he received Sumit's call at eight thirty in the morning. His official vehicle came around nine o'clock to receive him, so he jumped with the keys to his car and went straight to the bus stand. Mukesh was taken down from the bus, his body shifted to the city hospital ambulance and two media vehicles had also reached there.

Death of another suspect of the Jewar crime, within two days, was now stuff of media storm. His involvement in the murder of Bholaram's son could also not be ruled out.

Bholaram got ready and reported for duty to office on time. It was a normal day.

He knew that Sumit must have taken notice of him with the girl, but there was nothing to worry about. He would never be able to make out what had really happened.

One last hurdle remained. Bhure Lal had escaped from the city and was not on anyone's radar, not even of Sumit or Surender.

Sumit explained that a girl with a barrel almost like a flute was there at the bus stand and Bholaram was present there with her in civil clothes. Perhaps he had come to drop someone at the bus stand.

Surender could not understand. Hundreds come and go daily to the bus stand. Bholaram might have come to drop someone. How was coming to the bus stand a questionable issue? Did he take any action, no, then what?

His mind was reeling under pressure for Bhure Lal. Where was he now, where?

He was called to Lucknow. The same day a flight was booked for him by Krishna, his wife, who accompanied him as she wanted to meet her relatives in Lucknow.

Fifteen days had passed, with a storm of debates and accusations between Sumit Bhatnagar and Surender Nagar. Krishna was a silent witness to the rising heat with shouting voices from Lucknow.

77.

Finally tracking a chain of mobile numbers for six days, Sumit was able to trace Bhure who was again living at one of the semi-finished apartment sites in Greater Noida Extension.
Some of the workers were from his village and one supervisor decided to rent out a semi furnished apartment with a room cooler. He had been there for almost fifteen days.
One day the filtered water bottle delivery came late and reached by noon. With no bottled water nearby, Bhure drank some water from the water jug of a local tea seller and it caused a problem.
Bhure Lal was not well and suffered from diarrhoea. His condition was deteriorating and he needed to visit a hospital for a check-up. It was the same day that Sumit was finally able to trace him, spoke to him and decided to meet him in the night.
Surender was in a loop. It was a confidential message and they wanted no mistake in the whole affair. Some reliable persons of Surender had joined him for security cover.
They decided to get Bhure treated at the District Hospital in Noida, with proper security. Treatment in a private hospital was ruled out due to lack of money supply from Lucknow. They needed to come out of trouble, and it was the best option they could have managed in Noida without any help from any corner.

78.

Bholaram came to know of the whereabouts of his boss and Sumit as they went several times to the District hospital. The constable helping him informed him of the plan.
Both of them were now keeping a watch on each other, ready to strike. It was now a catch-22 situation.
There was security and cameras all around in the District Hospital. Bholaram knew the dangers and was not at all interested in

creating any problems for Ankita and himself.

Then the idea came to him. He rang his old friend and well-wisher at the District Hospital, Noida. He wanted to have a view from a hundred-metre distance with the window opening on the side of Bhure and that was easy.

Every detail of the room, location and site reached him. As a matter of practice, gastro patients were kept on the ground floor for treatment. One problem remained — the ground level was one metre below the ground floor level and Ankita and he could not get the view of the room behind the corridor boundary wall from any side.

He tried to understand the area in the evening. Some drainage work was progressing in the area and a surveying work for finalizing levels for laying pipes and construction of manholes was going on in full swing.

On Shobhit's request, Rahul Kumar also decided to help and both planned their positions.

Around eleven o'clock in the morning, Bholaram took a break to visit someone at the District Hospital. It was roughly three km away from his office.

Ankita was ready with her bag and reached on her own. She was part of the survey team. Three boys and two more girls were doing the surveying work since morning and were a part of the team, no one noticed or bothered.

Rahul Kumar was wearing an orange colour jacket, glasses and sports shoes. He looked like a permanent survey worker.

Ankita entered the hospital with a request to use the washroom and slowly moved towards the opposite of Bhure's open hall dormitory where other patients were also getting treatment.

Rahul and Shobhit coming from opposite directions intercepted her in between, just talking and laughing. Shobhit was carrying a hospital folder with test reports and x-rays, like a relative trying to find his patient in the hospital. He started talking to a nurse moving in the corridor asking some random questions.

He then entered through the open door, where Bhure was getting treatment, with glucose drips being given to him.

He came back and spoke about his position. It was a difficult proposition.

Bholaram was speaking with the police staff there and he walked away and pointed out the bed. It was not an easy location, the door was open, and three people were sitting around him. The angle at which Bhure was lying on the bed did not allow any access to his chest.

Ankita, with her mobile to her ears, seemed to be lost in some conversation like any other young girl of this generation who are always glued to their mobile phones.

After listening to Shobhit for some time, she changed the resonance frequency to a milder one and pressed the button on the tab, holding the barrel towards Bhure.

One minute later, Bhure was crying. He felt as if his digestive organs were burning up. He complained to the helpers nearby and they rushed to his help.

His stomach stopped all metabolic functions after the strike.

No one was there on the ground. Ankita, Rahul and Shobhit left but one thing remained as a clue. Bholaram was caught on the camera speaking to a constable on duty on some other case but he did not care.

Bhure kept crying in pain. Doctors found that his stomach was becoming rock solid. They kept pressing it and started giving medication. Five injections had already gone through the drip.

Suddenly his stomach caved in and became liquid due to cavitation.

Bhure Lal died the same evening and never went back to the protection of Surender Nagar. His three assistants were unable to explain, what really happened and kept reciting the conditions and doctor's efforts.

The post-mortem report baffled the medical fraternity. Stomach organs turning liquid, almost melted. How was that possible? Such a rare case.

There was terror in the eyes of Sumit and Surender. Everyone was being scanned, but nothing caught their eyes. Sumit kept crying hoarse about Bholaram, and he was told to keep a watch on him.

Bholaram was back on duty, with a smile, silent but nothing in his expression.

79.

Bholaram's presence in the hospital solved the puzzle for Sumit. Some machine was used in the elimination of all the three. He did not understand the nature of it and no one was capable of solving the mystery.

He discussed the matter with Surender in detail and informed him about Bholaram's involvement in the case.

Surender was convinced but how could they prove any of it? He knew Bholaram and about his goodwill in the department. All co-operation and silence were with him after his son's murder by the three.

Sumit was sure that since he was onto him, if they could be eliminated without a trace, his life was also in danger. Sumit understood it very well now, how it was all planned and exe-cuted. There was no proof, no trace, death from haemorrhage, heart attack or bad stomach could never be debated in the court, and then who could prove that some barrel worked. It was all a fanciful world of an unknown gadget.

Only one thing remained in his heart and that was fear. He now knew that Bholaram and Ankita both knew of his role in the pro-tection. That he was the mastermind, and the three relied on his skills to save them in the court.

He wanted a break. His favourite places were jungles and the sea-side and he liked journeying by train. They were always safer with their normal routine.

Sumit reached Surender's house in the evening with his laptop and office documents. They tried but failed and now a mystery remained. All the three died natural deaths, but how was it pos-sible?

There was a heated discussion between Sumit and Surender with Krishna hearing all the drama.

She knew that her husband had failed miserably at a personal task assigned by Hem Pratap Singh. There were many in the line, but the ramifications would be higher with the political connections of his father in law.

She also knew that only Sumit knew the whole story.

After receiving a mobile call, Surender stood up and ran to another room. He was trying to explain, almost pleading and begging.

Sumit felt the urge to go to the washroom and ran.

What happened, even Krishna could not understand. She felt the need to see the diary of Sumit lying near his laptop on the centre table. She picked it up and opened it. After five-six pages, there were several login ids and passwords.

She quickly opened the camera in her mobile and took a picture of the page, intuitively.

Sumit and Surender came back and sat on the sofa set. Krishna left them to bring some snacks from the kitchen. She heard her husband say, 'You should take a break and disappear from Noida immediately.'

'Yes, tomorrow, I am going.' Sumit ended the conversation.

After snacks and a single drink, Sumit left.

Surender and Krishna felt lost. How were they to solve the riddle when there was no clue?

Krishna raised a question, 'When all of them are dead, and they were wanted in the Jewar crime and for Bholaram's son's murder, would anybody care in Lucknow? Would they try to know who was behind these eliminations?'

'No one will care, it is a closed chapter now, either way they were a liability. The Chief Minister wanted to prolong elimination due to some election matters. There are many to replace them, all lined up. They will never want to know who was behind these cases. Then there is no murder, all of them died natural deaths. It is a boon in disguise.'

'And Sumit?'

'He remains a weak point for me.'

Tired and exhausted, Surender was back to drinking, almost feeling lost. This year had been very troublesome. He would like to lead a straight life.

Krishna opened her laptop in her room. It was almost midnight; her husband was still drinking unable to sleep.

She went to the pictures gallery and saw the captured image. There was one login id for IRCTC rail ticket reservation and password for Sumit Bhatnagar.

She opened the website and logged in, the details of the ticket booked for tomorrow's journey was available and she downloaded the pdf file. She called someone and asked for his e-mail id.

80.

With train being his favourite mode, he booked a seat in the sleeper class on Tatkal service as he could not find a better option.

Sumit thought he would find some solace in the journey and the break. The message had reached Lucknow, and there had been no reply. This time he had failed miserably, but with the assignment amount already transferred, he decided to keep quiet.

Bholaram and Ankita decided that for the final blow, it would be the ticket reservation information. The pdf ticket file reached Bholaram in the night sent by someone called Krishna Nagar.

Bholaram knew who she was. The smart wife, Krishna Nagar, understood that the wheel of fortune was against her husband. It was in his best interests that this matter closes here. Only Sumit knew what really had happened. She understood that it was Bholaram behind the deaths but how had he managed?

Bholaram and his team reached New Delhi Railway Station in the night itself and surveyed the area. Luck had favoured them. The seat allotted to Sumit was near the window on the platform side, as had been chosen by Sumit.

Bholaram in his civil dress finalized the location where Ankita would stand. Chances were remote this time as the time available was too short and there was no chance that Sumit would sit there at the right moment.

His car failed in the night, it did not start with all attempts and then came help from Rahul Kumar.

Driving 'Noida Express', the fateful Maruti Eeco, he made three rounds in the night from one o'clock until the morning hours—from Noida to New Delhi Railway Station—for discussions and planning by Bholaram, Ankita and Shobhit.

He did not utter a single word.

Bholaram reached with Ankita thirty minutes earlier. He stood there at the right side, some yards away, ready with his service revolver, for any action. He wouldn't need it, he understood that. Ankita was the only answer.Luck ran out for Sumit, as Ankita stroked perfectly.

Sumit recognised her face as he had seen her at the bus stand and had told Surender several times, that she was the one behind the deaths but why?

Santosh was waiting in the parking lot of New Delhi Railway Station. Bholaram, sitting by Rahul's side in the 'Noida Express', silently moved ahead with the memory of his son in his eyes.

Manju was relieved to bring justice to Nandkishor and his family.

Santosh did not utter a single word. He even decided not to look at Ankita who was sitting behind him.

81.

They came to know in the morning that Nandkishor's wife had passed away last night unable to bear the grief at eleven o'clock.

Her son, Rahul Kumar, did not tell anyone and ferried them in the night silently in the same vehicle of Rajpal's.

Manju brought the girl home to take over all her responsibilitiesin life.

Bholaram resigned from service the next day.

Surender Nagar was a changed person for ever.

82.

How the mystery was really solved for Ankita was not any wild idea or action. It was the humming of sound taught by Swami Shivanand that changed the game. It was the humming sound made by Ankita that made the barrel work. A unique sound to lock the device and operate it.

From those mythological stories of Devas and Asuras to modern research, everything had failed. Whatsoever she had tried did not capture the frequencies to make the radar work. When the radar did not capture the frequencies back in the system, how could the device have worked?

The riddle was finally solved by Swami Shivanand when she had come specially to meet him in his ashram a month ago. It took a three-day meditation session under strict supervision, chanting the mantras and reciting the sounds for hours. It was the sound lock that was matched with natural modulations that worked at last that made the radar work with it and it was further modified for a wide range of frequencies.

The family visited the monk after a month in Shiva Ashram at Gondal, near Rajkot.

Swami Shivanand was sitting silently and breathing deeply. Ankita kept her eyes closed while sitting in the room. It had been more than an hour, but there was no agitation in her.

One of the disciples entered the room. Swamiji opened his eyes and looked at him silently. The disciple left the room.

Swamiji looked at Ankita, turning his body in her direction to have full eye-contact.

'Silence is golden, and sometimes silence conveys more than all the words put together. It is always better to forget the past, Ankita. There is no witness of the past, and the future we never know of. Nature has not given us that power for a reason. Be at peace with yourself and strive for a purposeful life. My good wishes are always with you. Never have a feeling of guilt or sorrow for being part of a destiny you never anticipated. Be at peace with yourself, you will find the way.' Swami Shivanand again fell into silence.

Ankita folded her hands and bowed with respect. She came out of the room.

Manju was waiting for her in the Ashram's library. Both walked slowly and joined Santosh who was sitting under a tree.

———

www.ingramcontent.com/pod-product-compliance
Lightning Source LLC
LaVergne TN
LVHW091548170726
843492LV00007B/2094